Inn TheSpirit of Trickery

SPIRITS OF TEXAS
COZY MYSTERIES, BOOK 2

BECKI WILLIS

Becki Willis/Clear Creek Publishers
4253 CR 427
Marquez, Texas/ 77865
www.beckiwillis.com

Book Layout © 2017 BookDesignTemplates.com

Inn the Spirit of Trickery/ Becki Willis -- 1st ed.
ISBN 978-1-947686-08-3

Books by Becki Willis

Forgotten Boxes

Plain Roots

Tangible Spirits

He Kills Me, He Kills Me Not

Mirrors Don't Lie Series:

    The Girl from Her Mirror – Book 1

    Mirror, Mirror on Her Wall – Book 2

    Light from Her Mirror – Book 3

The Sisters, Texas Mystery Series:

    Chicken Scratch – Book 1

    When the Stars Fall – Book 2

    Stipulations & Complications – Book 3

    Home Again: Starting Over – Book 4

    Genny's Ballad – Book 5

    Christmas In The Sisters – Book 6

    The Lilac Code – Book 7

    Wildflower Wedding – Book 8

Spirits of Texas Cozy Mystery Series:

    Inn the Spirit of Legends – Book 1

    Inn the Spirit of Trickery – Book 2

CONTENTS

CHAPTER 1...1

CHAPTER 2...3

CHAPTER 3...15

CHAPTER 4...24

CHAPTER 5...35

CHAPTER 6...41

CHAPTER 7...56

CHAPTER 8...65

CHAPTER 9...73

CHAPTER 10...75

CHAPTER 11...80

CHAPTER 12...94

CHAPTER 13...100

CHAPTER 14...111

CHAPTER 15...113

CHAPTER 16...130

CHAPTER 17...133

CHAPTER 18...144

CHAPTER 19...156

CHAPTER 20...165

CHAPTER 21...169

CHAPTER 22...172

CHAPTER 23...179

CHAPTER 24...192

CHAPTER 25...1928

CHAPTER 1

"I want the trucks loaded and ready to roll, first thing Tuesday morning."

From behind his clipboard, the foreman nodded. "On it, boss lady."

"Any problems I should be aware of?"

"No, ma'am. The horses look good, the crew is pumped and ready to go, and even ole' Rusty is in good spirits for a change. Things are moving along slicker than an oiled pig in a mudslide."

"We have a lot riding on this show," the woman reminded him needlessly. "There's no margin for error."

"There won't be."

"Excellent. That's all for now, John Boy. Let's call it a night."

Two hundred miles away, a telephone rang, shrill and loud in the still evening air.

"Hello?"

"I need my money."

"About that…"

"No," the caller said. The voice was cold and flat. "I'm not granting you anymore extensions. You've had more than enough time to pay."

"I have most of it together. More than half. I just need a little more time to get the last few thousand."

"You have until Friday."

"I'll give you ten thousand by then, I swear."

"You owe me three times that."

"But I only borrowed twenty!"

"Interest, my friend." The caller's tone offered no hint of friendship. "I'll need fifteen, minimum, to renew the loan."

"But…"

"No buts. Fifteen thousand by Friday, or someone else will pay."

The line went dead.

The threat, however, was alive and real.

CHAPTER 2

The grand opening was fast approaching. In less than a week, *The Spirits of Texas Inn* would officially re-open and be back in business.

For Hannah Duncan, it seemed to take forever.

She did a mental checklist in her mind, going over the details for the hundredth time. On the plus side, with each new tally, the list dwindled. There were only a dozen or so items left on her immediate to-do list.

Confirm bookings. On her agenda for tomorrow.

Freshen all rooms. Definitely a last-minute detail, particularly the wildflower bouquets.

Order food. Technically Sadie's department, but she would oversee the process, just in case.

Conduct another trial run. Who knew when the forty-ninth mock check-in might reveal a weakness?

Meet with the farrier. He was due to arrive within the hour to make certain all horses were properly shoed and ready to ride.

Finish painting. Currently in progress, if the streaks in her dark hair were any indication. Just a bit more, and she was done.

Touch base with Walker. Okay, so she made that one up, just like she'd fabricate some flimsy excuse to see the handsome lawyer again. After having him underfoot for the first month she was here, she had gotten used to seeing him every day. It had been almost two weeks since she had last seen him and, strangely enough, she actually missed the maddening man. Surely, there was some document that required her signature or some loophole in need of tightening. *Something* to bring him back out to this silly excuse of a town she now owned.

Hang the rest of the rodeo posters. The colorful ads already plastered most of Fredericksburg and the communities fanning out from it in a twenty-mile radius. Fred promised to run a handful to Blanco and Wimberley. If she found time tomorrow, Hannah would take the last several over to Canyon Lake. The resort town drew plenty of tourists hungering for the flavor of Texas. What better filled that menu than a Wild West show and rodeo?

Hannah knew she was going on out a limb, hosting such a grand production on opening weekend. So much could already go wrong, without throwing a live performance into the mix. Not only were they working through the kinks of bringing the old inn back into service for the season, but they were doing it under new management. That, alone, might prove to be a circus.

JoeJoe, however, had taught her to dream big. Her uncle's motto was *'Go big, or go home.'*

In a crazy turn of events—orchestrated by the man himself and his twisted idea of unique birthday presents—Hannah *was* home. JoeJoe bought the tiny town of Hannah, Texas at auction and gifted it to his only niece for her thirtieth birthday. Like it or not, she was the new owner and operator of the historic inn. The only choice now was to go big.

She had discovered the rodeo company online. A few clicks, and she was intrigued. This could be just the draw she needed, the thing to single them out from the other properties in the area and make them shine. The thing to *Go Big*. If she were going out on a limb by operating the ancient old inn in the first place, she may as well go all the way out to the tip. Go big and fly, or fall and fail.

On the bright side, the old inn no longer looked quite so ancient.

If Hannah had little painting experience going into the project, she dared say she was now a borderline expert. Painting this room took her from novice to professional. Dry and thirsty, the original shiplap walls provided hours of hands-on experience. The first time she washed the boards with the creamy white paste, it soaked in faster than a half-inch rain on a dry prairie. The second coat hadn't fared much better. It wasn't until this, the third coat, that the color actually adhered.

It was amazing what a simple (or so the You Tube video claimed) coat of paint could do to a room. It transformed the tired old space into something alive and welcoming. The great room looked larger, and definitely more inviting. Against trim painted dark, inky black, the look was fresh, yet traditional. Historically accurate, but trendy.

Hannah couldn't bring herself to change the hardwood floor, other than to offer it a thorough scrubbing. She thought all those scuffed echoes from the past offered a nice contrast to the fresh promise of the new wall color. It was almost symbolic. A subliminal reminder, of sorts, to step from the past into the future.

If truth were told, it needed all the help it could get. Built in the mid-eighteen hundreds as a stagecoach stop, these old walls were soaked in history. Many a soul had walked through these doors.

The problem came when some of those *souls* couldn't bring themselves to leave, even after death.

How could the inn move forward, Hannah often fretted, when mired in the past with ghosts? Lucky for her, the spirits were friendly, but it was disconcerting to know an unseen entity roamed at will around her home. Perhaps the subliminal message would provide a gentle nudge and encourage the spirits to move along their way. One could only hope.

Going back to her list of things to do, Hannah worked her way around the room. She dragged a stool and paint pan along with her, doing touch-ups and yet one more application to the thirstiest of boards. She finally stood back to consult her work, a smile of satisfaction curling her lips.

It looked darn good, if she did say so herself.

Oops. One last spot, there near the window, before she could call it done. Hannah pulled her stool along. All it needed was a good stroke or two, just above arm's reach. If she stood on her tiptoes and stretched…

Got it!

She. Was. Finished.

With a proud and satisfied nod, Hannah lowered her heels back down onto the stool.

Too bad it wasn't there.

Unknowingly, Hannah had shifted just enough on the stool to alter her position. Turned just so, her heels came down onto nothingness. And with nothing beneath her, she began to fall.

She made a valiant effort to catch herself. Her arms went out for balance, but in doing so, the pan tilted. Paint dripped over the side and trickled down her arm. The brush did a catapult and landed with a fat, juicy *smack!* on her cheek. It then slid down the side of her neck and continued over the front of her blouse, leaving a creamy white swatch in its wake.

Hannah let out a yelp and tried twisting her body forward, but momentum had her headed the other direction. She knew she was falling, and there wasn't a thing she could do to stop it.

She heard a loud "Oomph!" as she collided with a warm, solid body. Strong arms came up to catch and hold her, paint and all, suspended in the air. Expecting to see Walker—and now, of all times, when she was covered in paint!—Hannah turned startled blue eyes toward her savior and prepared to thank him.

The words died on her lips as she stared at the stranger now holding her, his brown eyes alight with humor. Seeing the way his eyes crinkled in the corners, she was acutely aware of how close his face was to hers. She knew he was laughing at her, even before she saw his broad smile.

"That was some balancing act!" the man told her. "You should be on the high-wire."

She could think of no comeback. She was still too stunned to speak. First, from the fall, and second, from the fact he wasn't her attorney. This man was about the same height as Walker, but whip thin. He had a wiry strength about him, as proved by the way he easily held her in the air.

"'Course, without me or a safety net beneath you, that might not be such a good idea," he went on to say. His grin widened. "Did you paint the walls with that same technique, or just yourself?"

Hannah followed his eyes as they trailed down her neck and over her paint-smeared chest. She idly wondered if the paint was water-soluble or if her shirt was ruined. She was betting on the latter.

She finally found her voice. "Who—Who are you?"

"Shelton Long, at your service, ma'am." With his hands currently occupied, he couldn't tip his straw hat as he normally did. The best he could do was tip his head, hat and all.

"The horse shoe-er?" Hannah squeaked. From their phone conversation, she thought him at least twenty years older, nearer to fifty.

"That's one way of saying it," he agreed. "I'm a farrier by trade, ma'am. You must be my new client."

"Hannah Duncan." She attempted to put her hand out for shaking, but found her arm squashed between them. Only her fingers wiggled.

"That's okay. My hands are a bit occupied at the moment," he reminded her.

A dry voice spoke from behind them.

"They certainly are," Walker Jacoby drawled from the doorway. "Long, I knew you had a reputation for picking up ladies, but I thought the rumors were exaggerated." He let his blue eyes, stormier now than normal, wander over the cozy scene they created. "I guess I was mistaken."

Hannah twisted to see his face. From the tone of his voice, she knew he wasn't pleased. "Walker!"

"Whoa, there, little filly," the farrier warned, "or you'll have us both covered in paint." He was laughing at her again, but the look he threw toward the lawyer was sharp. "Jacoby, could you give us a hand? Even betwixt the two of us, we appear to be short-handed."

A notable pause revealed the attorney's inner turmoil. He was clearly tempted to snatch the woman from the other man's arms, but he eventually came forward and took the paint pan. He retrieved it from Hannah's hands and placed it safely on the stool.

When he turned back around, her feet still weren't on the floor. His voice came out sharper than intended as he snapped, "You can put her down now, Long. The crisis is over."

"Well, now, so it is," the other man drawled.

Despite agreeing, he was slow in relinquishing his burden. He was even slower in allowing her to slide down the long string bean that was his body. Hannah blushed, Walker scowled, and Shelton Long beamed like a lighthouse.

There was no salvaging her pride. Smeared in paint, Hannah looked, she was certain, like a fool. Worst yet, she had the distinct feeling the two men were using her as some sort of pawn in a game she didn't understand. The best she could do was make a hasty retreat and start over.

"Thank you, Mr. Long, for—"

"Shelton," he broke in, still wearing that silly grin. "After such an intimate greeting, I think we've earned the right to be on a first-name basis, don't you?"

She imagined the scene as it must have happened. His startled face when she came hurling into his arms, covered in paint. In spite of herself, Hannah felt a smile tug on her lips, as she continued her train of thought. She needed to do so fast, before she became completely sidetracked by his disarming smile.

"Thank you, Shelton, for coming to my rescue. But as you can see, I'm a bit of a mess, so if you gentlemen will excuse me…" She turned toward the still-brooding attorney. "Walker, thank you for preventing yet another spill. I'll change and be right back."

"No rush. In fact," the attorney offered, "I'll take Long out to the corral. Take as long as you like." He warmed to the idea as he relaxed his stiff pose. "You can even stay and finish your painting, if you like. I can handle this."

She ignored the thinly veiled ploy. Already headed for the stairs, Hannah called over her shoulder. "You two go on. I'll be out in a flash."

⸻⸻⸻◆⸻⸻⸻

Hannah didn't waste time taking a shower. The wet paint came off easily enough with a hard scrub, and her shirt could pre-soak for now. Leaving on the paint-dribbled work jeans, she pulled on a clean t-shirt and called it good.

By the time she reached the corral, the men were already at work. They examined each of the horses' hooves, turning them up and peering at them with knowledgeable eyes. One supported the horse's leg while the other scooped dirt and debris from around the shoe. The men worked together, but Hannah could feel the tension between them, even before she approached.

There was no denying the men were polar opposites.

With his raven-black hair and stormy blue eyes, Walker Jacoby was a handsome man in prime physical condition. Instead of the monogrammed western shirt and starched jeans Sadie called Walker's 'lawyer duds,' today he wore faded jeans a few wearings past their last starch and a close-fitting dark tee-shirt. This one touted a rafting outfit along the Comal River and left his impressive biceps exposed.

Handsome in his own right, the farrier was perhaps an inch or so taller than Walker, with wiry limbs stretched long and taut. Thin and angular, he was a study in sharp edges and lean muscle. His jeans were faded, stained, and ripped. The condition was clearly the result of use and abuse, not from some fancy manufacturer who slapped a ridiculous price tag on the look and called it fashion. His long-sleeve shirt was thin and loose fitting, enough so to offer ventilation, even on a day as warm as this. The pale-blue color, faded from countless washings, contrasted nicely with his suntanned skin and fair coloring. His blond hair was short and slightly lighter than the neat beard edging his face.

But, perhaps the biggest contrast between the two men was their personalities. Shelton Long had laugh lines around his eyes. Frown lines bracketed Walker Jacoby's mouth, at least in Hannah's presence. It seemed she and the attorney argued as much as they agreed. By contrast, she couldn't imagine having a serious argument with someone as friendly and affable as the horse farrier.

"Don't mind me," she said, self-conscious as both men looked up and watched her approach.

"You clean up right purdy, ma'am," Shelton Long said, exaggerating his thick Texas drawl and choice of wording. His eyes flicked over her with an appreciative smile.

Walker frowned. "Hannah, you need to see this."

With a sigh, Hannah came forward. She knew enough about horses to steer clear of the stallion's powerful hind legs. Even though he was gentle as a kitten, she was respectful of his strength. She leaned down beside Walker, who was crouched to support the horse's bent leg.

"Look at this."

Despite owning a prized retired racehorse by the tender age of seven—another of her Uncle JoeJoe's outrageous gifts—Hannah still had much to learn about the equine world. She knew, however, that the hooves were not supposed to flare that way, or to have chips and splits along the jagged edges. The dark, oily substance oozing from the center of the hoof wasn't normal, either.

She turned a worried face to the man beside her. "That's not good, is it?"

As Walker shook his head, the farrier answered, "I've seen a lot worse. This is what happens when horses go too long without proper tending to." There was a rebuke in his words.

"If you recall," Walker said in a stern voice, his gaze pointed as he addressed the farrier, "you broke our last appointment. This could have been addressed weeks ago."

Shelton shook off the criticism. "The important thing is, I'm here now. I'll scoop out the dirt and mud surrounding the frog, this triangular space here in the middle of his hoof. That black, oily residue is a sign of thrush, a bacterial infection that is common enough, but can cause a horse to go lame if not tended to properly. It's a good thing I'm here. I'll keep that from happening."

Hannah saw the spark of anger in Walker's eyes and knew things could quickly spiral out of control. She didn't know the history between these two men, but it obviously wasn't good. She deftly steered the conversation another way. "So, you can fix it?"

"Yes, ma'am." Shelton stood as he spoke, signaling the examination was over. "I don't see signs of abscess, but I suggest not riding him for a few days while the thrush clears up."

"But we have the trail ride coming up," Hannah fretted. She didn't want to endanger the horses, but she couldn't afford to be short one on their first outing. "I need all the horses in it."

"I can loan you a horse, if that's what you're worried about."

She visibly brightened. "You could?"

"Sure," the farrier grinned.

"That won't be necessary," the attorney ground out.

Both men spoke at once. Hannah's blue eyes bounced between the two.

"I'd be happy to loan you a horse," Shelton repeated.

"So will I," Walker interjected. "I always loan my horses to the inn."

"You do?" It was the first she heard of such.

His scowl deepened. "Fred knows the Rocking J supplies extra horses whenever you need them."

Fred and Sadie Tanner were institutions here at *The Spirits.* The maiden pair had lived their entire lives here, right alongside Wilhelmina Hannah. When their friend and benefactor died and instructed the town auctioned to the highest bidder, the sisters stayed on to help the new owner. Thanks or no thanks to JoeJoe Duncan and his strange sense of birthday gifts, that owner was now Hannah. She was eternally grateful for the older women's help and guidance. Without their wealth of knowledge and experience, she would be in over her head.

"She didn't say anything," Hannah murmured. "But good to know. Thanks." She smiled up at the attorney, and for a moment, it was just the two of them.

It was there again, that sizzle of awareness. It flashed between them like lightning, kicking Hannah's heart into overdrive and peppering her skin with gooseflesh. The spark of fire was inevitable whenever they were together, but Hannah did her best to ignore it. Though she tried to keep a professional distance between them—he was, as he so often pointed out, her attorney and executor of the convoluted estate in which she found herself embroiled—her traitorous mind couldn't help but wonder *what if.*

What if he had kissed her that night by the pond? *What if* they explored this undeniable attraction between them? When her body and her heart piped in with their two cents on the subject, the possibilities were limitless.

That was why ignoring the man was crucial. Impossible, but crucial.

As difficult as it was to do, Hannah turned away from the dark glimmer in his eyes and concentrated on the horse. Petting the velvety smooth coat, she struggled to keep her voice even. "So, the trail ride can go on?"

Shelton Long pushed up the brim of his battered cowboy hat and gave her a charming smile. "Well, we won't let a little thing like being down one horse stop it, that's for sure."

The relief was obvious on her face. "And the other horses?" she asked after a quick reprieve. "Or is Willie Nelson the only one in such bad shape?"

She had quickly learned that Wilhelmina used a rather odd but effective system for naming her animals. The chickens were named after a children's nursery rhyme, the cows bore the names of ice cream flavors, and the horses shared monikers with country music singers. Favorite literary and television characters inspired the goats' names.

"Well, let's take a look," the farrier said. With a flirtatious wink, he offered his arm in gallant fashion.

The echoing snort didn't come from the horse.

It came from the lawyer.

CHAPTER 3

By the time Shelton Long folded his lanky body back inside his truck and waved goodbye, all Hannah's horses were properly shoed, the farrier had none too subtly exchanged phone numbers with the innkeeper, a new spring appeared in Hannah's step, and Walker wore a perpetual scowl.

Pretending not to notice, Hannah turned back toward the inn. "Thanks for setting that up. I feel better, knowing the horses are in good shape and ready to ride."

"He backed out on me three weeks ago. I should have found someone else right then," the lawyer grumbled.

"I think he was a good choice. I liked the way he handled the horses."

"I just bet you did." He gave extra care to patting Leroy, the shaggy Great Pyrenees that came with the property. Sometimes, Hannah resented the bond between the giant white dog and the lawyer, but the two were old friends. Even now, Walker showed warmer regard for the dog than he did for the woman.

Hannah whirled around, her blue eyes flashing. "And what is that muttered remark supposed to mean?"

"Exactly what I said. The two of you seemed to hit it right off." The tone of his voice made it an accusation.

"He was very helpful, not to mention friendly. So yes, I guess we did hit it off." Her chin jutted out stubbornly. "Just like I hit it off with Sadie and Fred, but you didn't seem to mind that friendship so much."

"It's a bit early to call yourselves friends, don't you think? You just met the man two hours ago."

"Well, I do have his number," she reminded him. She wasn't sure why she taunted him, other than the fact his high-handed manner annoyed her. What did it matter to him who her friends were? "Maybe I'll call him up and get to know him better, before I declare us friends."

Walker all but growled in protest. "You don't want to do that."

Hannah propped her hands upon her hips and glared at him. "How on earth do you know what I want, Walker Jacoby? You barely know me, yourself. And you haven't seen me in two weeks. You can't possibly know who I do or do not want for a friend."

He remained steadfast in his argument. "I'm telling you, you don't want Shelton Long for a friend."

"Give me three good reasons why not."

"Because I know him, and you don't. The man's not what he first appears."

"Few people ever are. And that's two reasons, at best. Give me another."

"Trust me on this, Hannah. You don't want to get tangled up with Shelton Long."

"Oh, come on, you can do better than that. Give me one good reason not to be friends with the man. A *real* reason."

"I'm not at liberty to say."

His tight-lipped response gave her pause. "He's a client?" That puzzled her, because the two men didn't seem to care for each other.

"No."

Which could explain the negative vibe radiating off the men like a bad smell. "You've brought litigation against him," she guessed, making it more of a statement than a question.

"If that were the case—and I'm not saying it is— you know I wouldn't be at liberty to discuss it with you. Just take my advice and steer clear of the man. He's good with horses, but those skills don't necessarily carry over to people."

"Says Mr. Personality, himself."

Muttering to herself, Hannah abruptly turned and stalked toward the inn. She kicked at a small rock in her path. "If I didn't know better, I'd think he was jealous. But no, he's not interested in a relationship. It wouldn't be in my 'best interest.'" Even when talking to herself, Hannah used air quotes to emphasize her sarcasm. "If he can't give me a better reason than that, I may have to befriend Mr. Long, just to make Walker mad! It would serve him right. He may control my legal affairs—and yes, my money—but that doesn't give him the right to control my personal life. *I* control that!"

She had worked up a nice little fury by the time she reached the back door. She had such momentum going, she almost hated seeing the shiny red '53 Cadillac pulling in behind her. It was difficult to maintain her bad mood with the Tanner sisters around.

"Was that Shelton Long we saw pulling out just now?" Sadie asked, crawling out in another of her colorful moo-moos.

"Yes, he came to trim the horses' feet."

"It's about time! I told Sister that Willie Nelson's feet were in bad shape," Fred tsked. Popping the trunk of the fully restored convertible, she pulled out shopping bags.

In true Walker fashion, the man appeared in time to reach around the older woman. "Here. Let me get these for you."

Without relinquishing the bags in her hand, she nodded her gray curls toward the others still in the trunk. "There's enough to go around."

Easily filling his arms with the bounty, Walker couldn't resist teasing, "Did you ladies buy out the supermarket?"

Not for the first time, Hannah wondered why his teasing came so natural with the elderly sisters, when his manner toward her was often stilted and flat.

"Have to get ready for this weekend." Sadie's words were muffled as she pulled even more bags from the back seat. "We'll get the main delivery from Sysco tomorrow."

"You mean there's more food coming?" Walker made a face of mock horror.

"You know how I love to cook."

"That I do."

Hannah scooped up the last two bags and hurried ahead to open the door. Walker brushed annoyingly close as he hefted his bulky load through the narrow opening. She held her breath, hoping not to get another whiff of his intoxicating cologne. She swore he had the stuff specially formulated to enhance his own unique body chemistry, just to drive her crazy.

The scent trailed behind him, luring Hannah into the kitchen on his heels.

"You should have heard the buzz in town today," Sadie told Hannah as they worked together to stash the groceries. "Everyone is talking about the show."

"And the Grand Opening," her sister put in. "People are excited to have the inn back in business."

"Even though I doubt any of them actually stay here themselves." Hannah's tone was rueful.

"No, but that doesn't mean they don't support it. They tell out-of-town friends and family about it—"

"—and they attend our special events." The sisters had an uncanny habit of finishing each other's sentences, as Sadie did now. "Don't be surprised when they call to book meals here, too."

This was the first Hannah had heard about the meals. A startled look crossed her face, like a deer caught in the headlights. "We—We have a café, and you're just now telling me? Why haven't you told me this before?" She was already composing a list in her mind, of things she would need to get. Menus and wait staff, just to start.

"Not a café," Sadie assured her.

"But Sister is such a fine cook, everyone loves her food. We take a limited number of outside reservations for weekend brunches. Depending on how many overnight guests are booked, we can squeeze in an extra dozen or so local folk. And sometimes we'll host a special evening meal, just for fun. The townsfolk love those, don't they, Sadie?"

Sadie vigorously nodded her gray head as she beamed in agreement. One glance at Hannah's face, however, and her smile dimmed. "Oh, dear," she said in dismay. "We did it again, didn't we? We overstepped."

Hannah could hardly deny the claim. "It would have been nice," she said, trying to soften the sharp disapproval she felt, "to know about this before now."

"We forget, you know," Fred sighed, by way of apology. "It's just that after all these years—"

"—literally our entire lives—"

"—we've had a hand in running things. Wilhelmina depended on us to make and implement decisions, and

when we found something that worked, we just kept repeating it.”

Sadie nodded in agreement. “We forget we need
to run those things by you. That you’re the one to make
and implement the decisions now.” She tried to look positive, but her chin quivered, ever so slightly.

Hannah released a long-suffering sigh. More loyal
employees she would never find, but sometimes the sisters were, indeed, taxing. The last thing Hannah wanted to
do was hurt their feelings. She depended upon them just
as much as her predecessor had (if not more), but the fact
remained she was their boss, not the other way around.
They couldn’t spring things like this on her and expect her
to be fine with it.

“It’s not that,” she told them. Sometimes it was
difficult, straddling the line between being both a boss
and a friend. “But I didn’t budget for additional diners.”

“Oh, but I did,” Sadie assured her, her bright smile
returning. “The numbers I gave you included taking reservations. I bought enough food for a full house.” She
indicated the many bags of groceries still littering every
available space.

Understanding dawned upon Hannah’s face. “That
explains some of those odd phone calls this week,” she
realized. “When I told people we didn’t have a buffet,
they always asked to speak to one of you.”

Neither woman looked surprised. “We have a
waiting list,” Fred said, in her matter-of-fact way. “If anyone should cancel.”

“Which won’t happen,” Walker pitched in, “because everyone loves Sadie’s breakfasts.”

“So, you knew about this, too, but didn’t say anything?” Her tone with the lawyer was much more
accusatory.

"Know about it? I'm the one who came up with the idea, years ago," he boasted. "My family has been coming here since I was a kid."

"It's true," Sadie confirmed. "Back when he was still a little tyke, I would make him German pancakes and hopple popple casserole, and he would say they were so delicious, I should share them with everybody."

"I'd slip over here for breakfast, then go home and pretend to be hungry so I wouldn't hurt my mother's feelings," he recalled with a fond chuckle. "When she finally caught on to me, I begged Sadie to cook breakfast and let me bring my mother over for a special treat."

"His mother enjoyed it so much," Sadie said, "that he wanted to know if his friends could bring their moms, too. So, it started with Mother's Day—"

"—but soon blossomed into a regular event," Fred concluded.

Hannah stared at the lawyer, who seemed quite pleased with himself. "And you were how old?"

"I don't know. Eight, ten. Something like that." He shrugged nonchalantly.

Momentarily distracted by the breadth and grace of his muscular shoulders, Hannah snapped back to attention. "And you just ran around the countryside, at will." Her frown spoke volumes.

"Well, our land does back up to theirs," he offered.

"It does?" This, too, was news to Hannah. She threw up her hands in exasperation. "You live next door, and I'm just learning about it? What else have you been keeping from me?"

"I wasn't *keeping* anything from you," Walker denied. "You've never asked where I live. And it's not exactly next door. You access my parents' house from the highway, a good ten miles or so away by car, unless you go through the pasture. Which, by the way, is what I did when I was a kid."

"So, where *do* you live?"

"About three miles, that way." He used a box of crackers to point the direction. His sudden smile was disarming. "Why? You want a tour?"

She snatched the crackers from him to put them in their proper place. She attempted to do the same with him. "No, I do not. I'm much too busy to be touring anything other than this property. Which reminds me. We need to do one more trial run."

A round of groans circled the room.

"Hannah, honey," Sadie said, coming over and putting both her hands on the younger woman's shoulders. She gently pulled her away from the pantry. "Don't you think we've had enough trial runs? Everything is going to be fine. When that first guest checks in on Friday afternoon, it's going to go as smooth as silk. Don't worry so much."

"Easy for you to say. You've done this before. *I* haven't."

"That's what we're here for, sweetie," Fred assured her. "We've done this hundreds of times, and we'll be here, right beside you, helping until it's old hat for you, as well."

"We're in this together, dear," Sadie summed up her sister's sentiment as she administered a quick hug.

"Thank you." Hannah's wan smile still didn't look convinced. She heaved out a deep breath before thinking to ask, "Is there anything else you've forgotten to mention? We don't offer sky diving lessons, do we?"

"Don't be silly," Fred said with a dismissive frown. "Although in the rainy season, we have been known to have mud slide races. And of course, there's the spring crawfish boil, and the Halloween carnival each fall.

Oh, and the fishing tournaments, but those don't start until July."

"Wait. *What* fishing tournaments?"

The sisters managed to look contrite.

"Oops," Sadie said. "I guess we forgot to mention those, huh?"

CHAPTER 4

The caravan rolled in on Wednesday afternoon. By the time the eighteen-wheelers, horse trailers, food trucks, RVs, and pickup trucks converged upon the tiny hamlet, Hannah was close to panic mode. What had she been thinking, inviting such a huge operation to crowd into her tiny little town? And on opening weekend, no less?

Worry tagged along with her as she and Fred led them to the field behind the inn where they would eventually set up. At Walker's suggestion, the public wouldn't access the event through the town itself, but via the fence-line road at the edge of the property. Until he pointed it out, Hannah had never noticed the unattended lane, but she agreed it would be less intrusive for their overnight guests.

On the up side, Hannah decided, as she glanced back at the line of vehicles behind her, there would be no missing it now. Not after this caravan came through and dug an unmistakable set of ruts.

She and Fred waited for the lead eighteen-wheeler to idle to a stop beside them. They watched as a tiny woman, no bigger than Fred herself, jumped from behind the wheel.

"Now, that's my kind of woman!" Fred beamed proudly. The two were even dressed in similar fashion: fancy western duds, complete with boots, hat, and shiny belt buckles. "I like her already. Good choice, Hannah." She elbowed her companion in a show of approval.

"Which of you is Hannah Duncan?" the sprite of a woman asked.

Hannah stepped forward with an extended hand. "Hello. I'm Hannah."

"Jazz Dawson." With her tiny stature, pixie smile, pert nose, and a head full of short, blond curls, the woman actually resembled a sprite. "Nice to finally put a face with a name."

"Absolutely! And this is Fred Tanner. If you have any issues with the animals or the property, she's your go-to."

"Nice outfit," Fred murmured in appreciation. "Are those boots Lucchese?"

Jazz presented a foot swathed in rhinestone-encrusted black and turquoise leather. "Absolutely. Custom made to match the belt."

"Mine, too," Fred beamed.

"Is that a Texas Sweetheart buckle?" Jazz practically squealed. "You're not *the* Fredrika Tanner, are you?"

"The one and only."

While the two women exchanged an animated conversation, Hannah watched in bemused confusion. The best she could tell, Fred was once a trick rider and was still a bit of a legend in the rodeo and western show circuit. That explained the shiny silver belt buckle she always wore, even though the thing must weigh a ton and was almost as big as she was.

With the oohing and ahhing phase of the conversation over, the women discussed logistics. A middle-aged man with a dripping mustache joined them from the second semi-truck, who Jazz introduced as her show foreman, John Boy Hopkins. As they talked about the space required and the expectations of the show, Hannah felt the panic kick back in. She smiled and nodded in the appropriate places, but inside, her mind was spinning.

"Okay, so it looks like we're all set!" Jazz said brightly. "I have your signed contract and your deposit. We'll collect the rest at the gate and give you your cut at the end. Oh, just one last thing. I trust you have the insurance policies in place?"

"Yes, yes." Still practicing her deep-breathing techniques, Hannah nodded more than was necessary. "All done."

She hadn't understood why some of the policies were necessary, but she ran them by Walker before agreeing to purchase the short-term policies. He assured her that while some seemed to be a bit of overkill, it never hurt to be fully protected. There were the usual personal liability policies, covering guests and performers while on Hannah property. A few generic policies to cover equipment failure or damage, special-event coverage in case of inclement weather or unforeseen natural disasters. The final policies were on the animals, providing for adequate veterinary care and loss of income for the production company, should an injury occur and the venue be found liable. Walker combed through the policies, added some specific language for his own ease of mind, and signed off on each of them.

"Wonderful," Jazz said with a huge smile. "It's nothing but a mountain of paperwork, but it keeps my lawyers and my accountants happy." She clasped her hands together and looked around with twinkling eyes, clearly excited. "So? Can we get set up?"

It was now or never. Go big, or go home.

Hannah drew in an unsteady breath. "Yes, by all means."

"I don't mean to be rude, but it can get a bit hectic down here. You may want to watch from a safe distance," the tiny woman suggested.

"Oh, absolutely. Fred and I will get out of your way and let you get to work."

Jazz recognized the expression on her face and offered a wink of confidence. "There's no need to worry, you know. We've got this."

Even as the vehicles circled like a wagon train of old and set up camp within a tight circumference, Hannah nibbled on her lower lip. Would the open field to the right be enough room for parking? By the time the eighteen-wheelers unhooked and parked, would there be ample room available for patrons? Would there even *be* any patrons? What if all this was for nothing? What if the whole thing was a colossal failure? Clearly, *Hats Off Productions* had high expectations from her little town.

Calling Hannah, Texas a *town* was a bit presumptuous, by anyone's standards. What began as a stagecoach stop in 1851 swelled and waned over the next hundred and sixty-something years. At its height, the unincorporated town boasted some twenty or so families and enjoyed a healthy economy. In addition to the stagecoach inn and café, there was a blacksmith, general store, two saloons, one church, a gristmill, and a few other odd businesses sprinkled through time. One by one, the businesses shuttered, leaving only the General Store to remain on a come and go basis. That, and the faithful old inn. Despite numerous wars, the Great Depression, lean economies, and bad times in general, the *Stagecoach Inn* kept its doors open. About a hundred years into its lifespan, the name had changed to *The Spirits of Texas Inn*, but during all that time, a member of the Hannah family had owned and faithfully operated the property.

Upon Wilhelmina Hannah's death last year, the last of the Hannah bloodline was gone, and the family legacy ended. Her will instructed that the town and all its buildings, including the inn, be sold at auction. Hannah's uncle placed the winning bid and gifted it to his sole niece, thinking it amusing that she own a town bearing her name.

So now, here she was, knee-deep in panic, watching as organized chaos unfolded before her very eyes. A second 'town' was erected behind the first, almost a mirror image of how Hannah must have looked, back in the day. According to the false storefronts, this town also had a saloon, general store, blacksmith, and a dressmaker. She knew the string of make-believe buildings were a backdrop for the show, where the comedy acts, songs, and an Old West gunfight would take place. The portable pens were for the trick riding and rodeo-inspired portion of the program, and the food and game trucks were for the carnival alley.

Hannah had watched the video and studied the website, so she knew what the finished product should look like. But watching it unfold, all she felt was panic. As new worries washed over her, she wondered where to find the escape hatch.

"I think we should get back to the inn," Fred suggested, breaking into Hannah's pity party. "When we come back, it will be all set up and look completely different." She rattled on, trying to ease the younger woman's fears. "I've seen these set ups before, you know. They come in like a whirlwind and whip everything into shape. It's best to see the end result, rather than watch the madness."

"You're probably right." She still looked unconvinced, but she decided to take the advice and return to the inn. At least there, things were in a semblance of order.

Or not.

Hannah walked through the back door of the inn and promptly stepped into a pile of mushrooms. The squishy feel beneath her shoe startled her, causing her to jump away with a squeal. She landed on a head of lettuce, which masqueraded that day as a bowling ball. Hannah went down like a pin in a bowling alley.

"Holy boomtown!" It was a phrase her uncle had coined, born in the oilfields. "What *is* all this?" Her fall was broken, in part, by more scattered vegetables. They trailed down the hall, strewn from the kitchen to the back door. She had landed on a sack of flour, which softened the blow to her backside but resulted in a billowing cloud of white. The sack burst and flour mushroomed into the air like an atomic bomb.

"Hannah!" Sadie said in worry, hurrying into the hallway at the sound of such commotion. "Is that you? Are you all right?"

She struggled into a sitting position, pulling a sprig of parsley from her hair. "I think so. What happened in here?"

"The delivery man overturned his dolly when he high-tailed it out of here." Sadie huffed out a disgusted sigh as she extended her arm. "Here. Give me your hand, and I'll help you up."

"That's okay. I think I'll sit here a minute and catch my breath."

"You're not hurt, are you?" the older woman asked in worry.

"Just my pride. That wasn't one of my more graceful falls."

A giggle escaped Sadie's lips, pinched tight to squelch the sound. "You look like a ghost. You're all white with flour."

Hannah attempted to brush the powdery substance off her arms. "We have enough of those around here," she muttered, "without me joining their forces."

"Isn't that the truth! That's what caused this fiasco to begin with," Sadie told her.

"What do you mean?"

Fred, who trailed behind, stepped through the door and accessed the disaster with a shrewd eye. "What tornado hit in here?"

Her sister gave another noisy sigh. "Blackie Cole and Clyde Shumach."

The simple answer was enough to satisfy Fred. Without another word, she started gathering the scattered vegetables.

"Wait. Who's black as coal? Clyde Shumach? And isn't that a rather rude way of describing him?" She reprimanded the other woman with a severe frown.

"Blackie Cole," Sadie corrected. She took a wadded-up plastic bag from the pocket of her apron and tossed it toward her sister. It made it as far as Hannah and floated down atop her foot. "Hand that over to Fred, will ya? Clyde Shumach is the delivery driver. The one who heard Blackie say he saw a ghost, turned as white as one himself—like you are now—and skedaddled out the back door, spilling everything on his dolly as he mumbled prayers and obscenities, all in the same sentence."

"Did this Blackie person really see a ghost?" she dared to ask.

Sadie shrugged. "Probably. Clyde drove right over Caroline's yellow dress."

It was Hannah's turn to sigh. She didn't have time for this. *This* being resident ghosts and damaged food inventory. *This* being anything that stood between her and a smooth Grand Re-Opening, which happened in exactly two days' time.

Having not seen the spirits in the last few days, Hannah should have known it was too much to expect, thinking they would continue to stay out of sight. What if some of the guests saw them?

Which led to a new worry. *Could* the guests see them? Apparently, this Blackie Cole had.

Fred spoke as she worked on filling the plastic bag. "Clyde always has been a skittish young man. Makes you wonder how he ever handled bombs for the military."

"Maybe that's why he *is* skittish," Hannah pointed out. She brushed off her pants legs and attempted to stand, making certain there were no more dangerous lettuce bowling balls beneath her. Her gaze fell on the busted flour sack. "I hope we have more flour."

"No burs under my saddle," Sadie said with a nonchalant air. "That was a backup for my backup."

"What was Blackie Cole doing out here?" Fred asked.

Her sister motioned to the scattered produce. "What he does best. Making a mess. And by the way, he's still here."

"Then why isn't he helping to clean up his own mess?"

Fred was still grumbling when the door to the hall powder room opened. An unfamiliar man stepped forth, and Hannah realized the name 'Blackie' was as much a misnomer for this man as the tag Chicken Little was for the huge rooster outside. He had a full head of snow-white hair and bushy brows to match. Standing as he was in the doorway, the light behind him illuminated his long, white beard. With his pale skin tones, if Hannah didn't know better, she might think the man was a ghost, himself.

Or did she know better? She tried to replay the conversation in her head, listening for a clue. She gave a small shrug. He had opened the door, not walked through it as Caroline did, so she was going with the assumption the man was still among the living.

In lieu of a greeting, Fred demanded, "Blackie Cole, why aren't you helping with this mess you made?"

"Tweren't me who made the mess. Twas the delivery man," the old timer insisted.

"Because you told him you saw a ghost! Scared the poor boy half out of his wits!" Sadie cried in exasperation.

"I did see a ghost. Standing right there where you are, in a long, yellow dress."

"Have you been smoking grapevines again?"

"Haven't done that in years," the old man replied. "And don't act so high and mighty. You tweren't no better than me. You two done the same thing."

"Grapevines?" Hannah asked, perplexed.

Sadie's sheepish smile said she was guilty as charged. "They're hollow inside," she explained to the younger woman. "We used to light the ends and pretend they were cigarettes. Drawing that smoke into your lungs burned like the dickens, but made us feel all grown up and sophisticated." She struck a pose as she puffed on an imaginary stick and blew invisible circles into the air.

"Blackie was older than us," Fred pitched in, "and could smoke the real thing. But he let us tag along with him to all the best fishing holes, and we wanted to be like him and smoke. He turned us on to grapevines."

"Went to smoking them myself," he confirmed, "when I couldn't afford cigarettes."

"That's enough talk about grapevines. Help clean up this mess," Fred said.

"I would, but it's my back, you see." He put a hand to his bony hip, and his shoulders hunched more than they had just moments before. "Ol' Author has been writin' to me again." He snickered at his own joke. "Arthritis. Get it?"

As her companions groaned, Hannah stepped up and thrust her hand forward. "Hello. I don't believe we've met. I'm Hannah Duncan, the new owner of *The Spirits of Texas Inn.* How can we help you?"

"Well, howdy, there, little missy. You sure are a pretty little thing. But you don't look a bit like Wilhelmina. Ain't no one but a Hannah owned this here town since the middle of the 1800s."

"No, we're not related. And I didn't inherit the town. I bought it." She didn't bother with the technicality of her uncle having made the actual purchase. Explaining that fact to the older gentleman would probably take too long.

"How do you buy a town?" he asked, scrunching his face up so tightly it looked like a ball of white fur. "And *why*?"

"Good question," she muttered under her breath. "Can we help you with something, Mr. Cole?" she asked again.

"I came for dinner. I heard Sadie is cooking again."

"And I explained to him that we're not serving dinner, but the dang fool won't listen!" Sadie grumbled.

"I'm afraid you'll have to come back next weekend, Mr. Cole. Not this Saturday, but the next. We'll serve you breakfast then," Hannah promised. Having him underfoot on opening weekend was one complication they didn't need. She had a feeling they would have enough troubles of their own, without adding him into the mix.

It took several more minutes, but they finally saw the old gentleman off. They kept the conversation off ghosts and convinced the man he had his dates confused, insisting they weren't open until the following weekend. When he was finally gone, they finished picking up the strewn vegetables. Hannah stepped into the bathroom to wash residual flour from her arms, when someone knocked at the back door. She heard Sadie open it and have a brief conversation with the delivery driver.

According to the parts of the conversation Hannah could hear, the man realized he had overreacted and wanted to come back and apologize. He was happy to have the inn back on his route and hoped to make a good impression on the new owner.

Hannah was impressed with the gesture and wanted to commend the man on his professionalism. She guessed that the young veteran had served in the Afghanistan war, if what her friends said were true. Instead of spending valuable time washing the flour from her face, Hannah poked her head into the hall for a quick greeting.

"I know it was foolishness on my part," the man was in the middle of saying. "There's no such thing as ghosts."

Two things struck Hannah at once.

One, her friends' definition of a 'boy' and hers varied by about fifty years. If he were a war veteran, it was most likely the Vietnam War.

And two, for a grown man, he screamed like a baby at the sight of a real-live 'ghost.'

CHAPTER 5

He barged into the trailer without knocking. Offering no apologies and no greeting, he came right to the point.

"We may have a problem."

"Rusty again?" the reply came, sounding nonplussed by the sudden intrusion.

"I think he's getting suspicious. He's grumbling more than usual. Keeps asking questions, too, just like he did in Livingston. Why replace the turnstile counter? Why do we need this, why are we doing that? He didn't warm to the idea of doing it simply because his paycheck depended on it."

"I'll have a word with him."

The man continued with his complaints. "We don't need him grouching about everything little thing."

"This is Rusty we're talking about. He'd complain if we hung him with a new rope."

"His attitude is getting worse. And if he keeps this up, he's going to call attention to us."

"I said I'd talk to him. You just worry about things on your end."

He resented the reminder, as if he weren't a professional. "I have the turnstile set to drop a number, every thirty-two turns, so the head count could be off by a few. Dozen." He flashed a humorless smile. "In that case, the profits might be skewed in our favor."

"Do you think that's wise, in a venue this small? That's dropping four of every hundred tickets. You don't think they'll notice the numbers are off?"

"Would *you* notice the difference between ninety-six people and a hundred?" the man scoffed. "My eyes start to cross after I see a dozen or more of these yahoos."

"This is a smaller venue than we normally work," his companion reminded him, "so it needs to be handled with care."

"I'm aware of the smaller scale. That's why all the promotional posters are compliments of the show we did last fall in Crockett. The vet and feed bills are sponsored by the show out in West Texas."

"Year before last?" This, in surprise. "The information was still good?"

"Worked like a charm."

"Just be careful. If we get too greedy, it can jeopardize our entire operation. I advise holding off on using any more of our special sponsorships."

It sounded so much nicer calling it a *sponsorship* than what it really was: an outright scam.

"Fine. I advise holding off Rusty."

"Don't worry. I'll take care of Rusty."

***

Eyes glazed, the old cowboy wove a crooked path back toward the trailer, his stocky legs more wobbly than normal. He may have had a couple of beers too many, but it wasn't often John Boy was in such a generous mood. With the sets in place and the animals in prime condition, the show was poised and ready to go. The foreman had packed down his hundred-quart cooler with beer and ice, and offered it to the crew for a job well done. No reason they couldn't do a little celebrating tonight.

Rusty didn't know about the *celebrating* bit—it went against his grouchy nature, after all—but he was all for drinking beer. Even though alcohol had a tendency to enhance his dour outlook on life, he had a weakness for the bottle. He often suspected that money was the key factor standing between him and alcoholism, but on his income, excessive drinking wasn't an option. So, when someone offered it for free, he was more than willing to show his appreciation.

"Guess that's one advantage of workin' for pennies," he grumbled to himself. "Can't afford to drink all the time. One of these days, though, I'm gonna find me a job that pays better. I'm gettin' too dadgum old for all this movin' around."

He bumped into the side of his travel trailer, which appeared from out of nowhere. Shaking his head to clear his vision, he skidded along the metal siding until his shin met up with the front steps. He steadied himself before tackling that obstacle; those tiny stiles weren't meant for a size twelve. Good thing there were only two steps.

He paused on the top step and tugged the door open, immediately shielding his bleary eyes from the blinding light inside.

What he should have protected were his ears. The shrill scream that greeted him was like a knife to his eardrums, penetrating even the drunken stupor of his brain. When he jerked to cover his ears with both hands, Rusty lost his balance on the narrow step and toppled backwards. He tumbled off in slow motion, legs and feet tangling over his head, as Daphne Eland came to the door in nothing but a towel, shrieking her displeasure.

Still dripping wet from a shower, the leggy performer didn't bother checking on the man sprawled out in the grass. She slammed the door and locked it, her angry rant bleeding through the walls. Once again, the bumbling idiot had mistaken her trailer for his, and she was even less thrilled this time than all the times in the past.

By the time Rusty caught his wind and righted himself, the lights in the trailer went out, and he was left to find his way in the dark. He grumbled all the louder, complaining about the trailers all looking the same from the outside.

"It ain't my fault they put 'em in different order in every town!" He hiccupped between protests. "They should put 'em the same way, ever' time. One, three, four, and so on. Ain't my fault I walked in and saw her scrawny ole' chicken legs. Those things should come with a warning sign. 'Beware. Eyesore ahead.'"

Rusty reached the far trailer, immediately recognizing it as his own. Now that he thought about it, his had that dent in the door. Guy had kicked it in that night while he was getting lucky with that little buckle bunny in Athens. Apparently, his roommate didn't understand the significance of a locked door.

Come to think of it, Rusty admitted with another hiccup, maybe he himself didn't understand the definition of *getting lucky*. That gal was a good three hundred pounds of pure spite, and she hadn't taken kindly to his exaggerated claims of fame. She came back to the trailer with him to see his World Finals belt buckle, but when she discovered he won it in a poker game, she had stirred up quite a fuss. There wasn't much luck to spending the night alone, especially when the air conditioning seeped out a mangled door and tempers ran as hot as the thermometer. He and Guy straightened it out the best they could the next day—the door *and* the friendship—but both still leaked from time to time.

"Shoulda made Guy pay for a new door," Rusty grumbled, clumsily reaching for the handle. It took two tries before his trembling hand made contact. "It was his fault, not givin' me a little privacy. It ain't often I get a woman come back with me. I ain't full of looks and charm, like Ted and Tom. Their trailer should have a re-volvin' door, it gets fanned so often. All they gotta do is look sideways at a woman, and she falls into their arms." He shoved the door open, still complaining. "Boss Lady should charge rent for their revolvin' beds."

Stumbling inside, Rusty immediately stubbed his toe in the dark. "Bright as daylight in the other trailer," he groused. "Black as pitch in my own. Two roommates. You'd think one of them would think to leave a light on for a fella." He unsuccessfully groped the wall, trying to find the light switch. "And that's another thing. Why does chicken legs get a trailer all to herself, when I have to share with two people! Ain't fair. Iffen I ever did get lucky again, I'd have to make a reservation for my own dad-burned room." He was still grumbling when he final-ly found the switch. "Just ain't fair. Slick signs up with the production, and Boss Lady says he has to bunk with us. Ain't room for three in this tiny trailer."

Rusty squinted against the harsh glare of a single bulb. Neither roommate was home yet, despite the late hour. As long as they didn't wake him when they came in, he didn't care if they catted around half the night.

"Hope they didn't eat all the bologna," he said aloud, heading straight for the tiny refrigerator. "Knowing Guy, he made a pig of himself and ate it all. Then I'll have to go to bed hungry and wake up to his stinking farts."

His mood as sour as his stomach, Rusty belched as he peered into the tiny cavern. Just as he suspected, the bologna package was empty. Before he started on a new rant, his eyes fell on a bottle of his favorite beer. That hadn't been there earlier.

"Well, lookie here," he said. A seldom-seen smile cracked the corners of his mouth. "Ole' Guy left me an apology note."

Before the bottle was empty, the room went dark again.

CHAPTER 6

An insistent knock at the front door drew Hannah's attention. Glancing at the clock to confirm the time, she frowned. Why would someone knock? This was a public inn, for crying out loud. The doors had been unlocked since seven this morning.

Once again, she was perched on a stool, this time hanging curtains. The burlap window coverings were the perfect blend of rustic chic and stylish simplicity, as were the metal elements in the room. Depending on the eyes of the beholder, the tin and exposed metals were either industrial modern or early necessity. Steel rods held the tabtop curtains in place, bare pipes created artwork and door handles, and tin buckets and watering cans were repurposed as light fixtures. With a few final accessories and fresh wildflower bouquets—tied, of course, with raffia and twine—the look would be complete.

Hannah slipped the last curtain tab in place and fastened the rod into its holder, calling over her shoulder to whomever was at the door, "Come in! It's open!" She spread out the folds so that the material fell in a smooth line.

"I know it's early," Jazz apologized the moment she stepped over the threshold. The hesitant tone in her voice told Hannah she came bearing bad news.

With a sigh, Hannah abandoned her task. The other windows would simply have to wait.

She made certain her feet were on solid ground before turning to face the other woman.

Sure enough, Jazz's face was pale and pulled tight with worry.

"It's not all that early," Hannah contradicted. "But judging from your expression, I think this calls for coffee. Come on into the kitchen."

Jazz shook her head, setting her short curls into motion. "This isn't a social call. We have a problem. A tragedy." She tucked her hands into her back pockets and blurted out the news, "Rusty's dead."

Hannah blinked in surprise. She didn't remember meeting a Rusty the day before, but she was shocked, nonetheless. Just as Jazz obviously was.

"Here. Let's have a seat. And let me get Sadie and Fred in here, so we can all hear this together." She motioned toward the lounge area, where an assortment of chairs and benches clustered in casual groupings. Their newly upholstered fabrics were an eclectic mix of colors, textures, and styles.

Reluctant to leave the other woman alone in her time of distress, Hannah ventured only as far as the edge of the room to call for her friends. She hurried back to Jazz, who had taken refuge in a leather armchair and sat staring at the empty hearth. Murmuring her condolences, Hannah settled into its spotted cowhide counterpart and waited for Jazz to speak.

Sadie came from the kitchen, wiping her wet hands on a dishtowel. Fred tagged behind, carrying a silver teapot and polishing rag. The questions died on their lips when they saw the ashen woman sitting in the chair.

"Whatever is wrong?" Sadie asked, her face already scrunched in concern.

"Whatever it is, we'll fix it," Fred promised.

"You can't fix this." Jazz pulled her eyes from the fireplace, her expression stricken. "Rusty is dead."

"Rusty?"

"Our wrangler. He's indispensable. He cares for all the horses. He's part trainer, part vet." She rubbed her fingers across her brow. When she spoke again, her voice sagged. "He's more than that, of course. He's part of our family. He's been with us since the beginning."

"What happened?" Hannah asked. She hated to think of it at a time like this, but what if he had fallen victim to an accident? Would her insurance cover it?

Jazz lifted her shoulder in a shrug. "Heart attack, I suppose?" It came out as a question.

"Did he have a history of heart trouble?"

"Not that I'm aware of. With Rusty, it was hard to tell. He keeps to himself, mostly. Grumbles about everything, then goes off and sulks with a bottle." She scrubbed her forehead again. "Oh, listen to me, talking about him in the present tense. It's just so hard to believe he's gone."

"Of course it is, dear," Sadie said, patting Jazz's arm to comfort her. "No one ever expects these sorts of things."

A sad smile broke across the younger woman's face. "To be honest, I thought he was too mean and ornery to ever die. I never imagined he would be gone, just like that."

"When did it happen? And how?" Hannah asked.

"Sometime during the night, apparently. He shares a trailer with two other men. One of his roommates came in late, saw him there on the sofa, and assumed he was passed out drunk again. It wasn't until this morning that he realized Rusty was…" She seemed to struggle with saying the word *dead* again, so she comprised with, "…wasn't drunk."

"You've called the sheriff's office?" ever-practical Fred wanted to know.

The petite blonde looked stunned at the suggestion. "Why—Why would I call the sheriff?"

"An unattended death, of course."

"Oh. Oh, yes, of course. I—I wasn't thinking."

Sadie popped up from the red-checkered side chair where she sat. "You're clearly distraught. Would you like for us to report it for you, dear?"

"Uhm, yes, please. That would be very kind of you."

"I'll go call right now. How about I bring back a nice, strong cup of coffee? Or would you prefer sweet tea?"

"It's warm out already. I think I'd like iced tea," Jazz murmured.

"I'll bring some for everyone." Sadie slipped from the room, practically unnoticed despite her colorful Hawaiian shirt.

"Is there anyone else we should call?" Hannah asked gently. "His family, perhaps?"

"*We* were his family," Jazz said sadly. "He never married nor had any children." Her hands worked in a nervous gesture. "What are we going to do?" she fretted. "The show starts tomorrow, and now we're down a man. Not just any man, but our main handler!"

"Don't you have a backup? Someone who helped him?"

"We run a very lean operation. Everyone has a specific job, and they do it well. And yes, he has help when needed, but no one else knows the animals the way Rusty does. And reassigning someone as handler would mean leaving their position empty."

"Is there any way we can help?" Fred offered.

Interest flickered in Jazz's eyes as she seemed to consider the offer. Before Hannah could remind Fred of their own lean operation—just the three of them to manage opening weekend here at the inn—another knock sounded at the door.

Holy boomtown! What is it with everyone knocking this morning? Hannah thought irritably. She started to call out a greeting, but the door opened and a blond head poked through.

"Knock, knock," Shelton Long said, his face split with his customary grin. "Can a weary traveler get a room around here?"

Now wasn't the time for teasing, but he didn't know that. Hannah couldn't help the responding smile that curved her lips. "Sorry, all booked up."

"How about a big ole' glass of sweet tea, then?" His tone was hopeful as he doffed his hat and stepped fully into the room. "I was in the area and thought I'd drop by and check on— Oh. Pardon me," he said, interrupting himself when he saw the unfamiliar woman in the room. "I didn't realize you had a guest already. Is this a bad time?"

"Well—" Hannah said uncertainly, glancing at Jazz. The blond woman looked so forlorn.

An idea occurred to her, and suddenly, Hannah's face brightened. "Maybe not!"

Fred frowned in confusion, until Hannah continued, "You're good with horses, right? And know a lot about them?" She recalled the gentle way he had handled Willie Nelson.

"I'd like to think so, being as I make my living with them."

"How busy are you this weekend?"

It dawned on Fred where the conversation headed. She looked a bit skeptical at first, but eventually nodded her approval as Hannah picked up steam. "Because I think you may be just the man we're looking for!" Hannah shot off.

The farrier tried to look modest, but his smile was a bit too cocky to be convincing. "Well, that's always nice to hear from a room full of pretty ladies."

"Please, come on in." Hannah motioned him forward. "Let me introduce you to Jazz Dawson, owner of *Hats Off Productions*. They're the outfit presenting the show this weekend. Jazz, this is our local farrier, Shelton Long."

As the two shook hands and murmured polite greetings, Hannah went on, "Shelton, as it happens, is excellent with horses. I was very impressed with the way he handled our horses earlier this week, when he came out to re-shoe them. I think he may be able to help you with your predicament."

Jazz made the sounds of denial, but never quite finished her protest. "Oh, but—"

Hannah turned to the man who was now perched on a burlap ottoman, his long legs arranged like sticks in the cramped position. "Jazz," she explained to the farrier, "is in immediate need of a wrangler for the show. I know it's asking a lot, but do you think you could help her out?"

He was already shaking his head. "I'd like to, I really would, but there's just no way I—"

Hannah interrupted without apology. "There's been a sudden death. The show's wrangler passed away unexpectedly in the middle of the night. I wouldn't dream of asking you otherwise, but this is an emergency."

"Oh." He looked taken aback by the news. Reports of any death were always hard to hear, even when the deceased was a stranger. "Oh, I see." But the creases between his brows belied his words. The grooves deepened, as he asked, "No, I guess I don't. How could I help?"

Jazz was the one to answer, having apparently warmed to the idea. "I'm in desperate need of someone to feed and care for the animals, Mr. Long. Horses, mostly. We have a few skits with dogs, which Duke and Madge train and handle, and we have one llama. Like Hannah said, I know it's a lot to ask, but we're between a rock and a hard place. It's not just that we're down a man with no one available to care for the horses. We'll be taking an emotional hit, too, just as soon as the shock wears off." She blew out a deep breath, disrupting the curls resting on her forehead. "Right now, it still seems like a bad mistake. I keep thinking he'll walk in any minute, complaining about something." Her chuckle held more sorrow than amusement. "Rusty was a grumpy old cuss, but he was our old cuss. We'll miss him something fierce."

Shelton chewed the inside of his lip as he mulled over the situation. "What were Rusty's duties?" he asked.

"Besides caring for their physical needs, he prepped the horses for each performance. We have multiple skits in each show, but he never missed a cue. Rusty wasn't very good with people, but he had a real knack for horses."

The farrier pulled out his phone and scrolled through his calendar. "I reckon I could move a few things around," he thought aloud. "It's just for the next three days, right?"

"Four," Jazz corrected. "Today through Sunday. We pull out after the Sunday matinee."

"I don't know much about show business," Shelton warned.

"If you can saddle a horse, open a gate on cue, and hand the reins to each rider, you know enough to get by."

A slow smile broke out across his handsome face. "Well, then, ladies. It looks like I'm going in the show business."

"Really?" Hannah all but squealed. She had every bit as much at stake as Jazz did. "You'll do it?"

"I reckon I can give it my best shot. I can't leave you ladies in the lurch, not when I can saddle a horse as well as the next fella."

"You're a lifesaver, Mr. Long," Jazz said.

"Call me Shelton. And no, ma'am, I'm sorry to say I couldn't save your friend's life. But maybe I can make his death just a tad bit easier, at least during the show."

"Thank you, *so much.*" Jazz blinked away grateful tears as she placed her hand over her heart. "Seriously. You can't imagine what this means to me."

"My pleasure, ma'am."

"Yes, thank you, Shelton," Hannah agreed. "If you weren't willing to pitch in and help, we might have had to cancel the entire show, and then the grand opening would be ruined, and…" She stopped herself before she hyperventilated. "Needless to say, we owe you. Big time. How can we ever repay you?"

"Oh, don't worry," he said, throwing her a flirtatious smile. "I'll think of something."

Sadie returned with a tray of iced tea and a plate of cookies. "I called the sheriff's office. They're sending a deputy, the Justice of the Peace, and an ambulance right out."

"Not to sound crass, but I think it's too late for an ambulance," Jazz remarked.

"We're a small community," Sadie explained as she passed around refreshments. "We don't have a coroner on call, not like the big cities do. The JP will pronounce him dead. As long as the deputy doesn't suspect foul play, our volunteer fire department and EMS services will take care of the rest. "

"Like I said, Rusty's favorite pastime was complaining, but none of us took him seriously. No one would ever hurt Rusty, not on purpose," Jazz said with confidence.

"You can explain that to the deputy when he gets here," Hannah assured her. "Why don't you take a few minutes to collect yourself and unwind? I know you've had quite a shock this morning."

"To say the least. Thank you, for being so kind to me. And for understanding the predicament this puts us in." Her hand trembled as she lifted the glass to her mouth and took a sip of Sadie's tea, brewed up strong and extra sweet. "Mmm," she murmured in appreciation, allowing the dark concoction to work its way through her tense muscles. She seemed to immediately relax.

After a moment of quiet reflection, Jazz opened her eyes and remembered to thank the farrier. "And thank you, Shelton Long, for coming to our rescue."

"My pleasure, ma'am," he grinned, tipping his iced tea glass her way. "But there is one thing."

"And what's that?"

"I warned you I didn't know much about show business, but I know even less about llamas," he admitted.

"Don't worry," Jazz assured him with a bark of laughter. "Our llama thinks he's a horse."

***

Shelton stayed long enough to check on the inn's horses, promising to return later that afternoon to take on his new responsibilities. Hannah and Leroy met him at the corral as he finished, just as the ambulance pulled up to the inn. As Sadie told the dispatcher, there was no need for lights and sirens, or for hurrying.

"That's a real shame about that fella," Shelton said, watching as the deputy went out to greet the driver.

Hannah agreed with a solemn nod. "It's terrible. I don't think I even met him yesterday, but it's no less shocking. I guess that just goes to show, we never know when it's our time."

"Guess not. How'd Miss Jazz do with the deputy?"

"Fine, I guess. I tried to give them a little privacy as he asked his questions." They walked toward his truck, but both their eyes were on the other vehicles, now making their way across the pasture to collect the deceased.

"Found him there on the couch, huh? What a shame."

"I can't imagine how that must have been for his roommates, finding him there like that."

"And knowing they slept in the same trailer as a dead man," Shelton added, his voice low and ominous. "Gives me the willies, just thinking about it."

"Thank you, again, for stepping up and agreeing to help out. I know you have a full schedule and plenty of things to do with your own business, without squeezing in multiple performances out here this weekend."

"Who knows? It might be fun," he grinned. "It never hurts to build your resume, just in case." Instead of reaching for the truck door, he reached for her hand and smiled down at her. "Besides, I'd do just about anything to help you."

"Th—Thank you."

Shelton stopped and turned to face her, gently squeezing her fingers. "I know this might not be the best time, but I'd like to take you out sometime. Maybe we could go out for dinner, or to a movie." When she didn't immediately answer, he prodded, "Are you interested?"

Was she interested? Shelton Long was a handsome man, and he had such an easy personality. She found herself smiling while in his presence. He had called a few times in the past week, and she discovered that she enjoyed their chats. No doubt, a night out with Shelton would be fun and easy, and a nice diversion from the stress of the past few weeks. Or of the past few months, if she cared to go back that far.

When, exactly, was the last time she had a night of fun? Jill's bachelorette party? Back before the government seized the investment company she worked for. Back before she lost her job and most of her savings. Back before she came to Hannah to check out her uncle's latest crazy scheme and her unwanted birthday present.

Yet, she knew that wasn't exactly true. She may not have gone *out*, but there had been many fun evenings over the last two months. Sadie and Fred knew how to play a mean game of Rummy. Throw in Sadie's cooking and Fred's exploration with making wine and craft beer, and it definitely qualified as a fun evening. There had been other times, too. Movie nights with the sisters, curled up in her favorite easy chair, munching on popcorn and brownies. The night she filled in at Bunk-O, when the sisters hosted the monthly game at their cottage. Hannah was the only one there without gray hair, but the evening with fifteen highly competitive senior citizens left her winded and sporting scratches on her knuckles. As it turned out, some of those church ladies took dice rolling seriously, and didn't mind grabbing for stolen points.

There were quiet evenings when the sisters turned reflective and talked about the early years here at the inn, and some of their favorite and most colorful guests. Those evenings were always fun, because it gave her a glimpse into the past, and helped her imagine a new future here at the inn. And there were the nights down by the pond, when Walker brought his portable grill, and they dined beside the water. On two occasions, the sisters joined them, but that first night, it had been just her and Walker. That was the night he almost kissed her. The night he told her they could never be more than friendly business acquaintances.

So, why was it that she hesitated now? Strong, handsome, and fun to be with, Shelton was the kind of man she was normally attracted to. She *was* attracted to him. Maybe not in the rip-his-shirt-off kind of way, but in the get-to-know-him-better kind of way. She *wanted* to spend more time with him. Now was not the time to be thinking of Walker and wondering how he would react to her going out with the farrier.

"So, is that a no?" he asked, turning loose of her hand.

"No. It's yes. I mean, I—I am interested. In dinner or a movie. But…"

"But not in me?" His smile didn't quite reach his eyes.

"I didn't say that. It's—It's the timing."

Shelton looked toward the back of the property, where the production company was set up and where, even though they couldn't see it from here, the medics collected the body of Rusty the wrangler. "Yeah, I get it," he said, blowing out a breath. "My timing does kinda suck."

"Maybe after opening weekend," she promised. "And after things go back to normal. I mean, it's not every day someone dies on my property." A thought occurred to her, puckering her forehead. "Although with guests checking in here, what with their unknown backgrounds and medical histories, I suppose it's something that's definitely possible." Her mind drifted to new worries, which she murmured aloud. "I should talk to Walker about it; make sure our insurance policy covers natural death occurrences. In fact, maybe I should call him now, about Rusty." Hadn't there been a mention of such, in the packet of papers she signed for *Hats Off*?

From his lofty height advantage, Shelton looked down at her and frowned. "What's the deal with you and Jacoby?"

Her answer was quick. "He's my attorney."

"Yeah, but I think there's something more between the two of you than just that."

She didn't like the way he studied her reaction to his words. Her blue eyes flashed with irritation. "I don't know why you would say such a thing."

"Maybe because I just asked you out on a date, and your first instinct was to call another man," he pointed out.

"That has nothing to do with you asking me out. It has to do with that poor man who died on my property, and whether I could somehow be held financially responsible!" she snapped.

The farrier drew his eyes together in thought. "I don't see how you could be at fault. He died of a heart attack."

"We assume. For all I know, he was poisoned, or stabbed in the throat, or strangled to death."

"I think you're getting a might bit worked up," he said. He used his exaggerated drawl again, the one that made him sound country bumpkin and cowboy charming, all at the same time. He placed his hands on her shoulders and forced her to look at him between gulped breaths. "Breathe, darlin'. Take in a nice, deep, slow breath. There you go. That's better now, don't you think?"

His smile was contagious. Hannah forced herself to relax as her mouth curled in imitation. "I'm sorry. It's just I have a lot riding on this weekend. I wanted everything to go smooth and perfect. But here it is, one day before we even get started, and I've already killed a man!"

Shelton chuckled and pulled her in for a quick hug. "You didn't kill that man, missy. He probably had a faulty ticker. It's just one of those things. Tragic, but just one of those things. Most likely, the public will never even know."

Hannah pulled away, her eyes wide with newly imagined horrors. "The public!" she cried. "I hadn't thought about that! What will they think? What will it do to our reputation? Will anyone even want to come, once they hear—"

Hannah was clearly panicking. She was on a roll, spouting out one borrowed problem after another. It was the only way he knew to shut her up. Shelton pulled her to him and covered her mouth with his own, smothering her worries in an impromptu kiss.

The action shocked her into silence. After a brief break in her rant, she tried to speak again, to pull away and say something more, but he continued the onslaught of his mouth. By then, the kiss wasn't so shocking. In fact, it was rather nice. A few more moments, and Hannah found herself yielding to the unexpected pleasure of kissing Shelton Long. His hands slipped from her shoulders to catch her waist and hold her loosely against his long form. Just as Hannah reached her hand up to explore the curve of his neck and opened her mouth to welcome a more thorough kiss, a door banged behind them and startled their lips apart.

"Pardon me," Caroline said, floating out in her yellow hoop skirt. She fluttered a matching lace fan in front of her pale face. "Have you seen my beloved? He's in Company A, Gillespie Rifles, of the Third Texas Infantry. I can't seem to find him anywhere I look."

Hannah jerked away from the farrier, embarrassed to have been caught kissing him.

She shook her head, slightly amused at her own foolishness. Caroline was a *ghost*, for Heaven's sake, searching for her fiancé who died in the Civil War. Why should she care what a ghost thought? Yet here she was, putting a proper distance between her and the tall gentleman, and looking anywhere but at his eyes.

She did, however, sneak a peek his way. If he saw the apparition floating just a few feet away from where they stood, he made no show of it. He frowned, no doubt misinterpreting the negative shake of her head. It seemed easiest to let him think she regretted the kiss, than to explain a ghost had interrupted them. Besides, she wasn't all that certain she didn't regret kissing him back. No matter how nice it had been, she didn't want to encourage him. Not now.

"Thank you, Shelton, for calming me down."

A wry smile twisted his mouth. "I'd rather my kiss rile you up, not calm you down."

Hannah gave him a little push, flustered by his frank assessment of the situation. "You know what I mean. I appreciate everything you've done today, coming to our rescue with the show, and making me calm down and look at things reasonably." She tucked a tendril of dark hair behind her ear and dodged looking into his eyes. "I shouldn't keep you any longer. I know you have a ton of things to take care of, especially now since we've dumped all these new duties on you."

Instead of arguing with her, he willingly opened the truck door. "I do have a busy day ahead. I need to see as many clients today as possible, so that my weekend is free." He brushed his knuckles along her cheek, his eyes drawn to the lips he had recently kissed. "I'm anxious to get the next few days behind us, you know, so that we can pick up where we left off."

Hannah's only reply was a blush. Shelton was still laughing as he drove away.

CHAPTER 7

By the time Walker arrived, Hannah's nerves ran high again.

"What took you so long?" she demanded. She gave his boot just enough time to hit the ground before attack. Leroy danced around her feet, excited to see one of his favorite people.

"I was in Mason, with another client." She hadn't said what the matter was, just that she had an emergency. Glancing at the inn behind her, the attorney saw nothing amiss as he absently scratched behind the dog's ear. "What was so important you couldn't tell me over the phone? You aren't my only client, you know."

"I bet I'm your only client with a dead man on their property!"

"Dead man? What are you talking about?" Perplexed, he tilted his dark head. "Did Orlan do something to upset you?"

Orlan Varela was the ghost of a Spanish vaquero known to inhabit the property. To Walker's knowledge, the spirit was non-intrusive and always polite. He had helped save all of their lives when Hannah first arrived, so he found it surprising that she would now be upset with him. If anything, he was more a guardian angel than a haunt.

"I'm not talking about Orlan! I'm talking about Rusty Thompson, the show's wrangler who died here overnight. What if they file against my insurance? What if it was foul play, and they shut down the performance? What if the police put crime scene tape all around, and people are afraid to stay here? What if he had a virus of some kind, and the CDC quarantines the town? What if—"

"Whoa, whoa, whoa," Walker said, his tone gentling. "Slow down. Take a deep breath, and try to relax."

"Relax? How can I relax? Opening day is tomorrow! I can't relax!"

"Come here." His voice was somewhere between comforting and resigned. "It looks like you could use a hug."

Not even the most hopeless romantic could spin this into a seductive overture. There was nothing remotely romantic about the way he gathered her into his arms and gave her a perfunctory squeeze. Hannah had received warmer hugs from a sweater.

Despite the stiff gesture, she drew comfort from the feel of his arms around her. Walker was warm and solid, and exactly what her fractured nerves needed. She couldn't say why, but having him here made all the difference.

"A man died last night, Walker." Without the sharp lilt of hysteria, her voice was lower. Walker had to bend his head to hear the words muffled into his shoulder.

He still held her stiffly in an awkward embrace. Hannah's arms circled his waist, refusing to end this moment of comfort, no matter how meager. She felt his hesitation, and in the moment it took for him to yield, her heart crumbled.

When he blew out a long-held breath and relaxed against her, the crumbles didn't seem as disjointed. When he tightened his arms and pulled her in for a true embrace, she decided the crumbles were simply dust, knocked loose from her crusty emotions.

"Tell me what happened," he encouraged, continuing to hold her close. He somehow sensed that was what she needed now, more than his counsel.

Her hair brushed against his cheek as she moved her head in a slight shake. "I—I don't know. Jazz came in early this morning, white as a sheet, saying her main wrangler was dead. His roommates found him, still on the couch." Hannah stopped, wanting to relay the facts correctly. Had Jazz mentioned the couch, or Shelton? No, it had to have come from Jazz. She nodded this time, feeling more confident in her reporting. "They thought he was passed out drunk—which apparently has been known to happen—but didn't realize until this morning that he was dead." She squeezed his waist, daring to admit, "I know it's terrible. A man is dead, but all I can think of is how this will affect opening day."

"That's understandable," he assured her.

"No, it's not." She started to pull away, her voice a miserable wail. "What's wrong with me? I'm a terrible person! How can I think of myself and my business at a time like this? A man has died!"

He refused to release her, holding her steadfast within his arms. "Shh. You're not a terrible person. You didn't even know the man. It's natural to think about this in a non-emotional, rational manner." A smile lifted the edges of his mouth. "Although, I'm not sure how rational you were a few minutes ago. I'd say you were pretty close to being hysterical."

"I know," she admitted, relaxing against the arms clasped behind her. "It's just that I have so much riding on this weekend, and I wanted everything to be perfect. Then, first rattle out of the box, I kill a man."

"*You* didn't kill him, Hannah," he said. If she hadn't been so distraught, she might have marveled over the fact that Walker actually chuckled.

"That's what Shelton said," she sighed, "but I don't—"

He released his arms so suddenly, Hannah stumbled backwards. She cried out in surprise, catching herself before she fell.

"What was horse boy doing out here?" the attorney demanded, his blue eyes snapping. "Why were you talking to *him* about this?"

"Because he stopped by to check on the horses, just as Jazz was telling us what happened. And when I got a bit hysterical that time, too, he managed to calm me down." A blush crept into her cheeks when she remembered the exact method he used, but she refused to dwell on it. "He reasoned with me and told me it wasn't my fault. The poor man died of a heart attack."

"Then what was all that about police tape and quarantine?"

Hannah pressed her fingers just above her eyebrows, where a dull throb had begun. "Nerves," she admitted. "Hysteria." She dropped her hands and looked at him. His yelling would only make her headache worse, but she may as well get it over with. "I know you won't like it, but you may as well know. Shelton agreed to take Rusty's place in the show."

"*WHAT?*"

Funny how the reverberation from a single yelled word could ping-pong its way around in her brain and cause so much pain.

"What do you mean, he's taking his place?" the attorney bellowed. "What does Shelton Long know about show business? Who does he think he is, pushing his way in and taking over?"

"Please stop yelling," Hannah said, keeping her voice calm and low. "First of all, he didn't push his way in. In fact, *I* asked *him* to pitch in and help. And thank goodness he said yes!"

"*You* asked *him*?" He repeated the words as she had said them, but in a much harsher—and louder—voice.

"Stop staring at me like I have horns sprouting from my head!"

"Long is the one with horns," he hissed. "I wouldn't be surprised if the man wasn't the devil himself."

"I know you don't like him, but stop being so dramatic," Hannah snapped.

He refused to back down. His blue eyes were the color of a turbulent, churning thundercloud. "What on earth possessed you to ask *that man* to help?"

"I don't think you understand the seriousness of the situation."

He interrupted her before she could explain, sulking like a petulant child, "You're the one who doesn't understand. Long isn't someone you want to get tangled up with."

"You keep saying that, but you won't give me a reason!"

"He can't be trusted. I wouldn't trust that man any further than I could throw him. And with those long arms and legs sticking out in every direction, I couldn't throw him from here to there!" He jabbed a finger into the air, indicating a spot just a few feet away.

The pressure behind her eyes continued to build. She didn't have the strength to argue, so she went back to explaining.

"Without his help, we'd probably have to cancel the show. *Hats Off* has a very lean staff, with no one to pick up the slack for Rusty. Without a wrangler, there's no horses. And without horses, there's no show. No show means there's no entertainment this weekend. Entertainment that I advertised heavily across half of Texas, and was counting on to pull in a crowd. No crowd means no money. And no money means our opening weekend will be a complete failure!" She paused to pull in a ragged breath. "There!" she charged. "Are you happy? I'm hysterical again."

He was as relentless as a starving dog with a new bone. "No, I'm not happy. I don't want Long sticking his bony finger in where it doesn't belong."

Hannah pressed her fingertips against her eyelids. "Can you please forget about Shelton Long for a moment and concentrate on why I asked you to come out here?"

"I can, as soon as you tell me why I'm here."

Hannah would eat nails before she admitted that she had *wanted* him here, more than needed him. For whatever reason, she had known his presence would calm her down. Perhaps not her temper, but her unsettled nerves.

Instead of the truth, she fabricated an excuse. "I want you to look over the insurance papers and the contract with *Hats Off* and assure me that I have nothing to worry about."

"You have nothing to worry about."

"You didn't even look at anything!"

"Yes, I did. I looked over every single contract, every single paper, before you ever signed them. There's absolutely no way you can be held liable for a man dying of a heart attack."

"What if he was poisoned?"

"Unless you put Strychnine or some other deadly substance in his food or drink, you have nothing to worry about."

"How can you sound so calm?" It was an accusation.

"Because you have nothing to worry about."

"What if he had an airborne illness and they quarantine the town?"

"Then you have something to worry about, but not from a legal standpoint."

"So, you do admit, I have reason to worry!"

Walker put his hands onto her shoulders and forced her to look at him. "What's going on, Hannah?" he asked. "You aren't usually this high-strung. I admit, you had a similar reaction when you found out you owned a town that came with its own resident ghosts, but that was understandable. Who wouldn't freak out about that? But I watched you stand up to the Hatfield brothers. You were fearless in the face of danger. A man held a gun on you, but you managed to talk your way out of the situation." His voice gentled as he cupped her cheek in his large hand. "You didn't panic then. Why are you now? Why is this so different?"

"I'm not sure I can explain it."

"Try."

Her gaze drifted to the inn behind them. Long and lean, it had been constructed of limestone and hewn lumber over a hundred and sixty years ago. The two-story structure had weathered the years and the elements, mankind and modernization, yet it still stood strong and steady. It was a beacon in the community, not just to the has-been town of Hannah, but to the countryside as a whole. The old stagecoach stop had a history every bit as rich and proud as the rest of the Lone Star State. Each whitewashed board sheltered that history; each sandy stone anchored a piece of the past. And for Hannah, it held the promise of a future.

"JoeJoe may have bought this town on a whim, but to me, it's become more than that," she confided. "I studied investments in college, because it's what I knew. My father and uncle were always looking for investors for Duncan Drilling. I interned at *Lawrence, Schuster and McMahon Investments*, and somehow, I just never left. It was a good career, but it was almost as if it just… happened." She shook her head, turning reflective. "Maybe it came too easy."

"I happen to know you graduated with honors. That's not what most people classify as *too easy*, Hannah," he interjected softly.

"Don't get me wrong. I worked hard for my degree. I worked hard for the agency. But it was just something I *did*, not something I truly *wanted*." She glanced up at him. "Does that make any sense?"

"I think it does."

"I want this, Walker," she admitted, daring to bare her soul to this man. "I never thought it possible, but I've become emotionally attached to this place. To this inn, and this sad little excuse of a town. To the animals, and especially to Sadie and Fred. I want to make Miss Wilhelmina proud, and to carry on the legacy her family started, all those years ago." She looked him directly in the eye. "If I've learned anything from my impulsive, flamboyant uncle over the years, it's to give my all to a project. Anything worth doing is worth doing *better* than it has to be done. JoeJoe's motto has always been *Go Big or Go Home*." Her blue eyes took on a warm glow. "This is my home now, Walker, and I intend to *Go Big*. The thought of failing scares me to death."

"You aren't going to fail. You've got this."

His genuine smile almost convinced her, but there was still the matter of the dead man. "But what if—"

He silenced her with a finger pressed to her lips.

"No more 'what ifs,'" he told her.

"But—"

"No more 'buts,' either. With or without the show, you have a fully booked house. Most of them are repeat guests. They've been coming here for years without the promise of entertainment, and they'll keep coming back for years, with or without that promise. The town, and the area, is entertainment enough."

"I suppose you're right." The words, spoken against the finger still at her lips, lacked conviction.

"I'm always right," Walker said with a smug smile.

She stuck her tongue out, pushing his finger away. "You are so full of yourself," she complained. "You'd better be right about this. Jazz better not be able to sue me."

"Who, by the way, is this Jazz person you keep mentioning?"

"Jazz Dawson, owner of *Hats Off Promotions*. You probably recognize her by her legal name, Jasmine. Right now, she's still in shock over Rusty's death. I just don't want the shock to wear off and the greed to set in. Some people are sue happy, you know." She pierced him with her look, as if his position as a lawyer made him re-sponsible for all lawsuits.

Walker released a weary sigh. "If it makes you feel better, I'll look over the papers. *Again.*"

"Actually," she replied smartly, "it would. And af-ter that, maybe you should meet Jazz. It wouldn't hurt for her to know I have someone looking out for the town's best interests."

CHAPTER 8

Hannah convinced herself it was the cookies that made her feel better. Sadie had brought out another plate of macaroons while she and Walker holed up in the office, looking through contracts and insurance policies. Alternately, she reasoned that it could have been Walker's legal expertise, and his assurance that, after combing through the paperwork to confirm what he already knew, she had absolutely nothing to worry about.

It couldn't possibly have anything to do with inhaling his unique scent, or listening to the strong, smooth cadence of his voice for the past hour. It couldn't be his mere presence that made her feel decidedly better. No, she stood by the cookie theory. They had to be responsible for her shift in spirits.

By the time they headed for the show set, Hannah felt no lingering traces of hysteria.

"Wow, this is quite impressive," Walker said with a low whistle, expressing his approval of the makeshift 'town.'

"I agree," Hannah said.

It looked one hundred percent better than it had when she saw it yesterday, proving Fred right. Watching it go up had been nerve wracking, but seeing the finished product gave her a surge of confidence. Maybe, just maybe, everything would work out, after all.

Portable bleachers flanked the row of wooden storefronts, allowing prime visibility of skits and performances. More than enough speakers and lighting strung through the air to ensure the audience an enjoyable experience. The rodeo arena and holding pens wrapped around the left side of the stands, and to the right was a string of food trucks and carnival-like game trailers. Beyond that were the eighteen-wheelers, RVs, and trailers needed to run an operation of this capacity.

"I don't see how people on the far side of the bleachers will see what's happening in the arena," Walker said. "It's going to be hard enough for the ones on this side. They'll have to crane their necks or sit sideways."

"Look again. See that platform the stands are on?" Hannah pointed to the massive steel circle under them. "It turns. The whole thing's like a giant lazy Susan. After the skits, the stands turn this way, so that the audience can watch the rodeo portion of the program."

Looking suitably impressed, Walker nodded. "Very smart." He gazed across at the food trucks, reading their brightly colored banners. "I see they have all the prerequisites for a carnival. Kettle corn. Cotton candy. Corn dogs. Fried everything."

"And don't forget funnel cakes. They're my favorite."

When she stumbled on the uneven turf, he put a hand at her back to guide her along. They turned toward the food trucks by silent accord, even though none were open yet. Hannah knew that Jazz's RV was the fancy one directly behind her preferred treat.

"That's something I worry about," she confided.

"The funnel cakes? What, are you worried you'll eat too many and gain a pound?"

"Sadie's cooking has already done that. And I've gained more than just a pound, I'm afraid." She laughed breezily, before turning serious. "But no, I'm not talking about the funnel cakes. I worry about the uneven ground, and people falling."

"You worry too much. And if the worse should happen, and someone does fall, that's what the extra insurance policy is for."

"I guess."

The wide break between the 'town' and the food trucks led directly to the backstage area and the trailers beyond. Hannah knew that during show times, orange netting would keep people from snooping in the restricted space, but for now, the netting was cast to one side. As they approached, the sound of a woman's laughter drew their attention. They looked up in time to see Jazz and Shelton Long stepping from the front RV.

"Speak of the devil," Walker muttered. She felt his muscles tighten, even though his hand barely grazed her back. She could feel the tension seeping into the air.

"Try to behave," she said out of the side of her mouth. Jazz saw them and waved them over, her expression much brighter than it had been this morning.

Hannah could swear that Shelton wore a guilty expression on his face, but she couldn't imagine why. Then she remembered the kiss, and assumed he was afraid she would think something of seeing him step from another woman's personal trailer. In truth, it never occurred to her to be jealous. He would be working for Jazz, at least for the next few days. It was only natural they had business to attend to. And if it turned out to be more than business… Hannah wasn't sure she *would* be jealous. The kiss had been nice enough, but she had all but forgotten it in the course of the day.

"Hannah, I'm so glad you came! Look who dropped by to learn the ropes." Jazz motioned to the man behind her.

"I hope we aren't bothering you. I wanted to introduce you to someone," Hannah said. "Jazz, this is my attorney, Walker Jacoby. Walker, this is Jazz Dawson, the dynamo behind everything you see here."

"Nice to meet you," Walker said, extending his hand for a cordial greeting. The nod he issued the farrier was far less welcoming. "Long."

"Jacoby," he returned with equal coolness.

"It's a pleasure to meet you," Jazz cooed, placing her other hand upon Walker's. The gesture effectively pulled his attention back to her, as she clung to his hand and went on about finally meeting the man behind the emails.

Hannah watched the exchange with pursed lips. *Okay, so maybe she was jealous, after all.* Just over a different man.

"I was sorry to hear about your wrangler, Miss Dawson," Walker said, gently tugging his hand free.

"Please, call me Jazz. We're all one big family around here. Which, of course, is why Rusty's death hit us so hard." A shadow crossed her face, puckering her pretty features into a frown. "But we're also professionals, and we know that the show must go on. Rusty would expect nothing less from us."

"Has the sheriff's office released the scene?" Walker asked.

"Yes. They finished their investigation about an hour ago, and gave us the go-ahead for tomorrow night. It appears Rusty died of natural causes or the bottle, one of the two. Either way, they've taken down the tape and released the trailer back to his roommates."

"Who were his roommates?" Hannah asked, for no reason in particular.

"Guy Woods and Pierce Maldonado. I think you may have met Pierce yesterday. Tall, dark, and handsome." She wiggled her eyebrows and then smiled up at Walker. "Actually, he reminds me a bit of you, Walker. I can call you Walker, can't I?"

"Of course."

Hannah didn't like the flash of jealousy that slammed through her, any more than she liked the stupid smile that curled Walker's lips.

Behind his new boss, Shelton sneered at the attorney's reaction to the petite blonde.

"I don't know what we would have done if Hannah hadn't suggested Shelton." Jazz spun unexpectedly and caught the farrier's arm, almost catching him in the act of openly mocking the other man. "Most likely, we would have had to cancel the shows. Thank goodness, this man came to the rescue. He's a true god-send for us."

It was Shelton's turn to preen beneath her praise. "You haven't seen me at work yet, ma'am," he reminded her.

"Hannah says you're excellent with horses. Her endorsement is good enough for me."

Now Hannah felt like a heel, being jealous over a woman who was so genuinely nice and flattering to *everyone*. Flirting just seemed to be her nature.

"I was just about to take Shelton around and introduce him to the rest of the crew. Would you two like to come along?" Jazz offered with a bright smile.

"Sure," Hannah answered for them. She was familiar with some of their names and faces from the website, but nothing compared to meeting each person in the flesh.

Hats Off did, indeed, run a lean crew. It didn't take long to make the rounds, meet the entire entourage, and hear about the multi-functions they performed. Some were in the middle of practice or necessary preparations, while a trio of them shared an afternoon beer and swapped stories about their late cast mate. From what Hannah could determine, most of them viewed Rusty as a crusty and grumpy old uncle, the kind you tolerated more than enjoyed, but the kind you cared about, all the same. Everyone seemed saddened by his passing.

"You remember John Boy Hoskins, Hannah. You met him yesterday." Jazz made the introductions to the burly man who barked out orders to anyone who would listen. He had done the same thing yesterday, for the little time Hannah had been around him. "Shelton, you'll report directly to John Boy or me. Some of the others may try to give you orders, but ignore them. This man or I are the final authority."

As they moved along, Jazz explained, "John Boy is my general manager and right-hand man. He oversees set up and take down and helps with training. Employees, not animals," she clarified. "He's also the emcee for the event, and on some nights, he helps at the gates. Hannah, you remember that you'll need to supply one attendee at the gate for each performance? I've found it's best to have two people, one from our side, one from the hosts, to as-sure that everyone's happy. That way there's no misunderstanding about how many people came through, or how the money was handled. And of course, we have a counter on the turnstile, for the official count. That's how you'll be paid. Fifty percent of the entry fee for every per-son through the gate. Once we reach capacity or the show starts, whichever comes first, the gates close and attend-ants are free to move on to their other tasks. For John Boy, that's as emcee during the show, security after-ward."

"What events do you have?" Walker asked.

"We do several comedy skits, including the one with dogs, a few musical numbers, and a Wild West gun fight. During the rodeo portion of the show, we do barrel racing, stunts, mutton busting, and trick riding."

"You never mentioned sheep," Shelton said stiffly.

Jazz looked unconcerned with the oversight. "All you have to do is open the gate, let them in, and then herd them out again. Petro takes care of the sheep. Kids from the audience ride them. It's a crowd favorite."

"And the dogs?" he clarified.

"Duke and Madge Artledge, the married couple I introduced you to. They train, care for, and perform with the dogs. They also sing duet, and work the food and carnival trucks. Because of our lean crew, the carnival is only open before and after the show. Likewise for the food trucks. At intermission, we sell drinks and popcorn in the stands. Because of safety issues around the turning grandstands, we try to keep our audience seated as much as possible."

"Sounds wise," Walker said. No doubt, his head swam with dozens of potential litigation issues surrounding the giant turntable.

"I still don't see how *that* few of people," Hannah motioned to the crew in general, "do all of *this*." She motioned to the stage and the carnival trailers.

"We all wear multiple hats," Jazz assured her. "As our main wrangler, Rusty was one of the few people who had a singular job. But with animals being the main focus in our performances, even in some of the comedy skits, it's arguably the most important job of all. Which is why you have been such a *huge* lifesaver, Shelton. Without a proper wrangler, our show would fall apart." She beamed up at the lanky blond man.

"That sounds like a lot for one man," Hannah remarked.

"Yes, it is. Our gopher Jeff helps him, but there are so many other tasks that demand his attention. His brother pitches in from time to time, but Guy is our electrician and mechanic. When something breaks down, or when the turntable needs rotating, he's the man. And Pierce is excellent with the stock, but he has his own duties. His good looks make him a natural for the gates and the carnival games. During the show, he's one of our lead actors and performs stunts during the rodeo."

"What kind of stunts does the cast perform?" asked Walker.

"Daphne has a high wire act, Pierce does roping and trick riding, as do I, we have a chuck wagon sequence, and Talia plays with fire."

"Plays with fire? Isn't that dangerous?"

"Stunts are always dangerous," Jazz said. Her smile widened and she took Walker by the arm, her eyes a-twinkle. "That's what makes them so much fun, don't you think?" She tugged him toward the row of fake storefronts. "Come. I'll show you the behind-the-scene secret to some of our most popular skits. One hint: trap doors, so watch where you walk. Or lean, as the case may be."

Seeing Hannah's confusion, the petite blonde laughed aloud in delight. "It's all about trickery, my friend. Things are seldom as they seem."

CHAPTER 9

The phone rang, breaking the stillness of the night. "Hello?"

The caller did not bother with pleasantries. "Do you have my money?"

"It's not Friday yet."

"It's almost midnight."

"You never specified a time."

"Fine," the caller said. "12:01. AM."

"But—But that's in three minutes, at best!" This, in a flash of panic.

"Very well. Another five thousand will buy you a twenty-four hour extension."

"That's twenty thousand dollars by tomorrow morning."

"Ah, you *can* count. Don't forget to add the interest penalty. You now owe me forty grand."

"That's double what I borrowed."

"Your mathematical skills continue to astound me."

There was a brief lull, accentuated by a painfully loud gulp of courage. Then came a daring move. "I have a proposition for you."

"*You* have a proposition for *me*?" the caller scoffed. "Need I remind you? You are hardly in a position for bargaining."

"This is no bargaining tool. And certainly no bargain. This could be worth millions."

The caller allowed a pregnant moment, ripe with the palatable threat of silence, to tick away. "I'm listening."

"I may have just stumbled into the opportunity of a lifetime. I'm sure you're familiar with the name Joseph Duncan, of Duncan Drilling?"

"Of course."

"I may have an inside track to his Achilles' heel. His favorite—and only—niece. Hannah Duncan."

The voice on the other end of the line was cold. "You have five minutes to make your pitch. Don't waste my time."

CHAPTER 10

Friday morning dawned bright and sunny. At least the weather seemed to be cooperating for opening week-end.

Hannah's nerves had returned in grand fashion, but a huge bouquet of yellow roses was the soothing balm she needed. Before she could call Walker and express her appreciation, he walked through the door.

"Walker! The roses just arrived. I love them!" She beamed from beside the fragrant bouquet, her smile as bright as the sunny petals. "Thank you so much."

He wore an odd expression upon his face. "The roses aren't from me," he told her.

"They're not? But who—" She dug through the leather leaf, until she found the hidden card. Reading the brief note, she knew exactly who had sent them.

Break a leg. (Not literally. It's part of this new show-biz lingo I'm learning.)

"Never mind," she murmured. Tucking the card away, she attempted to change the subject. "What brings you by this morning? Fan of train wrecks in the making?"

"No, I came to bring you these." He looked slightly embarrassed as he pulled a simple but elegant wildflower bouquet from behind his back. "I know it's not as fancy as roses. And I know you ordered similar bouquets for all the rooms." He thrust the flowers forward, his voice softening. "But these are for you."

Her face pinked with pleasure, and tears misted her eyes. "Thank you, Walker," she said softly. "That was very thoughtful of you."

"They're not as flashy as roses," he grumbled. He knew exactly who had sent them.

"No, they're not," she agreed. "These are so much more perfect. I love them." The soft glow on her face confirmed the words.

When Walker rubbed the back of his neck, Hannah knew he came bearing bad news.

"You may as well just say it." Her voice was resigned.

"Say what?"

"Whatever it is you're working up the courage to say."

"How do you know I'm working up to say something?"

"You always scrub the back of your neck. I hope you don't do that in court. The opposing counsel will immediately know when you're bluffing. Or when you're not sure of your position."

He jerked the offending arm down, his expression one of *guilty as charged*. "I try not to," he murmured. "But you're right. I am working up to say something. The flowers aren't just a wish for good luck. They're also a peace offering."

She narrowed her blue gaze to study him. "And why, exactly, do you need to offer me a peace offering?" A horrible thought occurred to her, widening her eyes into giant orbs. "It's the insurance policy, isn't it? They're going to sue us for Rusty's death!"

Walker scowled at her melodramatic response. "No, nothing like that. I came to tell you that I'll be out of town for the day. There's a sensitive legal issue I must handle immediately, and I have to go to Abilene."

"Oh. Of course." She made a shooing motion with her fingers. "There's no need for you to be here today. The real test doesn't start until tonight, when the guests arrive and the first performance begins."

"That's the thing," he told her, his voice solemn. "As much as I would hate to miss it, there's a good possibility I won't be back until late tonight."

Hannah blinked, absorbing the bad news like a physical blow. She knew it was irrational, but she felt as if he were letting her down. She realized then how much she depended on him and his silent strength. Like yesterday, just knowing he was present made all the difference. How could she get through opening night without him?

The disappointment was plain on her face, even though she tried to hide it.

"I'm sorry, Hannah," he said, stepping closer. "If there was any way I could postpone this, I would. But it is paramount I go today."

Her voice was subdued. "Of course. I understand." She did understand. She knew she wasn't his only client. Despite his active involvement in her estate, it was only natural that other clients would take precedence from time to time. Hannah had no doubt he wouldn't go if it weren't important. "I'm disappointed, of course, but I do understand."

Walker remained close, reaching out to touch her cheek. "I'll do my best to get back here in time for the show," he promised, voice low. "I'm sorry I won't be here for you."

Her first instinct was to say, 'it's okay.' But to do so would be lying, so she said, instead, "Don't rush on my account. Do a good job for your client, and drive safely." She touched her fingers against his hand as she spoke.

It was a daring gesture on both their parts. Both knew it was a poor excuse for the kiss that could never happen.

His dark-blue gaze danced with hers, slow and sincere.

"I'm sorry."

"Don't be."

"I am. I know how important today is for you. I wanted to be here for you. To share it with you."

Her smile was sad. This was probably the most personal thing he had ever said to her, the closest he had come to saying he cared. Not as her attorney, or as the executor of the estate. Not as a social connection, or as a friend. The simmering glow in his eyes, and the low timbre of his voice, revealed that he *cared*.

"You'll be with me in spirit."

"Absolutely." His fingers trailed away from her cheek in a gentle caress, setting off delightful shivers all through Hannah's body. His smile caused a hitch in her breathing. This was a smile just for her.

Stepping back, he put space between them. Otherwise, he might never say goodbye. "Call me if you need *anything*. I'll be in meetings, but I'll return the call as soon as I can."

"I will. Definitely."

"You promise?"

He obviously had trouble leaving. Hannah gave him a gentle shove. "The sooner you leave, the sooner you can get back here," she pointed out. "And the sooner I can get back to work."

"Right. Okay." He took a few steps of retreat. "Well, good luck. Keep me posted on how things are going."

"I'll try to limit it to major catastrophes and shining victories," she promised with a smile.

"Good plan." He finally turned around, taking his first steps toward the exit.

He was halfway to the door when Hannah called his name. He turned to see her hurrying across the room.

"Thanks again for the flowers," she said, brushing a quick kiss across his cheek.

The image of his pleased smile stayed with her through the rest of the day.

CHAPTER 11

By one o'clock, Hannah had checked, rechecked, and re-rechecked her list a hundred times. As impossible as it seemed, there was nothing left to do. Everything was done, with time to spare.

"I knew we could do it, girl," Fred said with a confident smile.

"I couldn't have, not without you two," Hannah assured them. "You ladies are amazing. As soon as Walker comes home, I'm telling him to give you both a raise."

"It's a shame that boy couldn't be here today," Sadie said, genuine sorrow in her voice. "He's been such an important part of this place for so long. It doesn't seem right, having opening night without him."

"I know, but he had to go to Abilene. It must have been something important to make him miss this," Hannah agreed.

"He's involved with the university there, you know," Fred said. "On the board or some-such panel. Every so often, he has a meeting he can't miss. It's just a shame that it happened today, of all days."

"Walker is on the board of a major university?" Hannah asked in surprise.

"Don't let the small-town image fool you, dear. Walker Jacoby is as smart as a whip, and quite accomplished for a man so young."

"He'd make quite a catch for some lucky woman," Sadie put in. She none too discreetly cut her eyes toward Hannah.

"I suppose some women are out fishing," Hannah conceded, "but not this one. So get that look out of your eyes and banish that thought from your head." To signify the matter closed, Hannah clasped her hands together with a loud pop. "I think I'm going to wander out back and see how things are coming with the show. Anyone care to join me?"

"I've got a cake in the oven," Sadie said, shaking her gray curls.

Fred also declined the invitation. "I want to stay close to the front desk. Check-in doesn't start until three, but you never know when someone will show up early."

"Okay, I won't be long. Call me if you need me." Hannah waved her cell phone at them before tucking it into the back pocket of her jeans.

While things were quiet at the inn, nothing could be further from the truth at the *Hats Off* site. To Hannah, it seemed that a hundred things were happening at once, giving new meaning to the phrase 'like a three-ring circus.' This was a condensed version of the entire show, played out simultaneously.

Inside the arena, the lovely Talia Petrosian stood barefoot upon the back of a magnificent Arabian stallion, twirling a baton. Flames flared out from either end of the shiny stick as the horse galloped around the ring.

Behind the stands, Duke and Madge practiced with their team of trained dogs. Hannah counted five Dachshunds and one hound dog. All were long and lean, with floppy ears and sleek red coats. Hannah laughed when she saw the hound dog shrink its large body and slip through a long, narrow tube behind the weenie dogs.

A gunfight was underway in front of the string of storefronts. Heedless to their shouts of bravado, Ted McCavish sat behind them, strumming his guitar and crooning out a sad western ballad. His voice was surprisingly good. With his talent, not to mention his looks, Hannah had no doubt he would be welcomed on much bigger stages than this.

She spotted Jazz and John Boy having an animated conversation with the darkly handsome Pierce Maldonado. Jazz used exaggerated hand gestures to get her point across and John Boy scowled heavily, but Pierce's expression caught Hannah's attention. For a man in a heated discussion with his immediate superiors, he looked oddly calm and confident. If the cocky smile playing upon his lips was any indication, he fared quite well in the match up.

Hannah was hesitant to intrude on the conversation. While she stood back and debated approaching, she saw John Boy throw his hands up in exasperation and stalk away. What she saw next shocked her, although it shouldn't have. Besides, it was none of her business. Hannah watched as Jazz ran her hand up Pierce's arm, a cajoling smile working across her lips. He frowned at first, but when she stepped closer, he couldn't resist. He swept her against him and gave her a hard, passionate kiss. Hannah felt the steam all the way from where she stood.

More reluctant than ever to intrude, Hannah started to turn away. Before she could quietly melt away into the shadows, she saw Shelton Long approach the couple. Obviously, he had no so such qualms about intruding upon their private moment. He launched into an immediate conversation with his new boss. Their expressions struck

Hannah as amusing. Jazz looked un-fazed by the interruption (and about being caught lipped-locked with a member of the cast), Pierce looked aggravated, and Shelton seemed oblivious to it all.

Pierce soon huffed his displeasure and stomped away, his exit drawing attention to Hannah.

"Oh, hi there, Hannah!" Jazz called, her smile bright and inviting. "Come on over. We're just making last-minute adjustments."

Hannah returned the smile. "All I can say," she told the other woman upon approach, "is '*wow*.' This place is hopping today!"

"Crunch time," Jazz agreed, following Hannah's gaze around the busy grounds. "Time to work out lingering bugs and put the final polish on each performance. How are things up at the inn?"

"Quiet. I think we're all set." Not wanting to ignore the man who politely stood by during their exchange, Hannah turned to smile up at the tall farrier. "And how are things with you, Shelton? Are you getting the hang of your new gig?"

"I think so. It's different, but I always enjoy a challenge."

Hannah wondered if he might consider *her* one of those challenges. Something in his knowing smile said he did.

"He's doing great," Jazz said with genuine enthusiasm. "You were right; he has a real way with horses. I didn't think anyone could take Rusty's place, God rest his poor soul, but I stand corrected."

"Hey, I'm just temporary help," Shelton reminded her. "I like what I do, where I am, and who I work with." His eyes slid over Hannah, openly flirting with her, as he drawled, "I ain't going nowhere."

Hannah looked embarrassed, and Jazz laughed.

"I'd offer to let the two of you be alone," Jazz teased, "but there's work to be done. Hannah, where's that handsome lawyer of yours? I promised to show him my routine."

I just bet you did. Green fangs of jealousy curled around Hannah's heart. "Unfortunately, he had to go out of town on business. He's not sure he'll even make it back in time for tonight's opening show." For the first time, Hannah thought that might not be such a travesty, after all.

"Oh, no! That's terrible!" Jazz said, looking crestfallen. Hannah had no doubt she meant it. Despite her involvement with Pierce, Jazz was clearly attracted to Walker.

And who wouldn't be? Hannah reasoned. Like it or not, even she suffered from the affliction.

"That's too bad," Shelton agreed, but he made no effort to sound sincere. "He's going to miss all the fun. But don't worry. I'll be here, Hannah, if you run into any trouble. Don't hesitate to call me if you need anything."

"I think you'll be plenty busy, yourself," Hannah said, covertly nodding toward Jazz. Did he need reminding that his new boss was standing right there, listening to him pledge his help?

"After the show, of course," he said promptly, resuming a professional air. He straightened the beanpole that was his body and addressed his boss in a serious voice. "Which brings us back around to that problem I was telling you about. I'm really concerned about that mare."

Jazz was thrown by the sudden shift in conversation. "Problem?" she blinked in confusion.

"You know, the mare. Tilly, I think is her name? She's practically the star of the show, but I sure don't like the way she's limping this morning. I think you should come take a look at her."

"Oh. Oh, right. Of course."

"Hannah, will you hang around while I show Miss Jazz what I'm talking about?" Shelton asked, touching her arm. "I wanted to talk with you, but this really can't wait. We may have ourselves an emergency."

"That doesn't sound good," Hannah worried aloud. She motioned them away. "By all means, go take care of the horse."

"You'll wait?" Shelton reaffirmed.

Hannah nodded her agreement. "I'll watch rehearsals."

He winked as he sauntered off with the other woman. Despite his claims of urgency, his long stride looked relaxed and unhurried as he crossed the grass. Beside him, Jazz made three steps to his one.

Hannah wandered back to the western town. With the gunfight over, the actors had moved on to another skit, this one a comedy. She laughed at their jokes and imagined what the audience would think of it. If they enjoyed the show even half as much as she enjoyed rehearsal, the evening would be a wild success.

"Enjoying yourself?"

The deep voice startled her. Hannah snapped her head around to see Pierce, lounging against the bleachers where she sat.

"Yes, I am," she smiled. "Everyone is so talented."

They exchanged idle chitchat, discussing the show and the various jobs some of the performers covered. When the conversation lulled, Hannah said, "I was sorry to hear about your roommate. I know that must have been quite a shock."

Pierce shrugged his shoulders. "It's a shame, but I really didn't know him that well."

"But you shared a trailer, isn't that right?"

"We were assigned to the same trailer," he agreed. The same cocky smile she had witnessed earlier spread across his handsome face. "That doesn't mean we have to sleep there."

She wondered if he spent most of his nights in the flashy RV up front.

"It's a small trailer, and with those two hotheads going at each other all the time, it was a bit crowded for my tastes. They claimed to be best friends, but with friends like that, neither needed enemies. I avoided staying in there any more than necessary. Besides," he supplied, "I haven't been with the crew as long as most. Less than two years."

"Oh? What did you do before that?" Hannah asked.

"I worked a magic show in Vegas."

"Magic?"

While the concept was intriguing, it brought flashbacks of her tenth birthday. From where he stood slightly below her, the man watched the emotions play across her face.

"That's an interesting reaction. You look like you might cry," Pierce pointed out. "And yet, you're laughing."

"Am I? I was just remembering my tenth birthday. I wanted a magic kit, so my uncle took me to Vegas to see a live show. Everything was great, until they called me on stage to be 'sawed' in half." She laughed aloud at the memory.

"What kind of uncle takes his ten-year-old niece to Vegas for her birthday?" Intrigued with the story before she even answered, Pierce swung his lithe body onto the bleachers and took a seat, uninvited, next to Hannah.

Caught up in the memory, Hannah thought nothing of it. "JoeJoe is not your typical uncle. He's definitely one of a kind."

"JoeJoe? Sounds like a kid, himself."

"A big, silly, impulsive, overgrown kid," she emphatically agreed.

"If he took a kid to Vegas for her birthday, I'm guessing he's either a gambler or very rich."

"Guilty, on both accounts."

Pierce studied her for a moment. "Wait. Your name is Duncan. You're not talking about Joseph Duncan, are you? Oil mogul and poker player extraordinaire? "

She looked at him in surprise. "You know my uncle?"

He continued to stare at her. "Your uncle is Joseph Duncan." From the sound of his voice, he seemed to find it impossible.

"Yes. Although to me, he'll always be JoeJoe. You know him?"

"Yeah. Yeah, I do. Or I did." Still looking stunned, Pierce went on to explain, "Before I did magic, I worked the high roller tables in casinos. Your uncle was a regular. Man, I've never seen anyone play the game the way your uncle does! He's legendary."

"Yes, that would be JoeJoe." In spite of the sarcasm, there was true affection in her voice. She adored her uncle.

By the time Pierce relayed a few funny stories involving her uncle, they laughed together like old friends. Her first perception of him and his cocky smile didn't jive with the witty, personable man beside her.

"So, how do you go from high stakes poker to magic?" Hannah wanted to know.

"It's the same thing, really," he said with a shrug. "It's all about making things disappear. Money, bunnies, one half of a birthday girl…"

"Ah, don't remind me!" she said, giving his arm a good-natured slug.

"Easy, there," he teased, rubbing the spot she had barely grazed. "That's my shootin' arm."

"That's the biggest leap of all. Poker, to magic, to a Wild West show. What's next? Opera?"

"If I ever attempted that, I'd make an entire audience disappear, I'm afraid. No, I think I'll stick to the skit in the show."

"You do a magic trick?" Hannah asked in surprise.

"Just small stuff," he assured her. "Our most popular skit involves the audience. We get someone to come up from the crowd, and we do a little skit with them. There may or may not be magic involved." As he said the word magic, he did a fancy motion with his hand.

"Hence, the trap doors Jazz mentioned yesterday," Hannah murmured in understanding. She looked around, realizing how much time had elapsed. "Speaking of Jazz, I wonder what the holdup is. I'm supposed to be waiting on Shelton, but I need to get back to the inn."

"Are you and Long an item?"

"No. I just recently met him. I liked the way he handled my horses, so I suggested him as a fill-in for your friend." Hannah glanced at the clock on her phone and stood. "If you see him, would you tell him I had to get back?"

"You can tell him. He and Jazz are coming this way now."

They were deep in conversation, concern evident in their faces. Jazz rubbed her forehead, a gesture she seemed to do when she was nervous. Like Walker's neck rub, it was a definite tell. Early on, JoeJoe had taught Hannah the importance of interpreting the silent signs people gave off. He said it was a useful talent to have, not just in poker, but also in life in general.

Shelton was the first to look up and see them sitting together in the empty bleachers. The scowl on his face was obvious, even to the casual observer.

"You may not think you're an item," Pierce said out of the side of his mouth, "but Long certainly does. If his eyes were weapons, I'd be a dead man right about now."

Jazz, on the other hand, looked more worried than jealous.

According to them, the news wasn't good. The mare came up lame that morning, favoring her front right leg. Even after several treatments, she showed no signs of improvement.

"I don't know what we're going to do," Jazz worried. "To train another horse on such short notice is impossible."

She paced, drumming her fingers to her forehead. "You've done an excellent job so far, Shelton, but let's give credit where credit is due. Rusty had every one of those horses trained to perform on cue. You're able to step in and take his place because, even though the horses aren't familiar with *you*, they're familiar with the routine. There's no way we could bring in a horse who doesn't know you, doesn't know the routine, and expect it to perform well." She paused long enough to turn on her heel and reverse her steps. "As you know, a horse not only has to know the routine, but it must feel comfortable with its handler. You wouldn't have time to establish a rapport with another animal. You would need to build trust, and confidence, and a sense of familiarity with the animal. No, we need another solution."

They all threw out suggestions, all of which were soon rejected. Jazz talked about the routines in the show and the specific training required of the horses. Pierce finally gave Shelton a shrewd look and said, "Long, you have horses. According to all that bragging you've been doing, you have the finest barrel racer in the state of Texas. It may not know all the routines, but it knows how to run barrels, and it knows you. The way I see it, that's half the battle."

Jazz stopped her pacing to look back and forth between the men. She wore a hopeful expression. "Would that work? Do you have a horse you could bring in? Pierce, you may just be brilliant!"

"Of course I'm brilliant," he smirked. "What about it, beanpole? You claim she's the smartest horse you've ever seen. Are you willing to put your money where your mouth is?"

"My horse is twice as brilliant as you are," Shelton snapped, his manner brusque. Clearly, there was still some lingering antagonism between the men. "She can pick up any routine, anytime."

Jazz clasped her hands together in delight. "Then we can use her?"

The tall man suddenly looked unsure. "Oh, now, I—I don't know about that."

"If you're chicken…" Pierce goaded.

"I ain't no chicken! My horse can do anything any one of yours could do! And she'd do it better, too," he boasted.

Jazz ignored their bickering. "Then it's perfect!" she cried in delight. "If she's already trained to run barrels, and she's as smart as you say, she could easily take Tilly's place in the show. Shelton, go get your horse and—" She stopped mid-sentence and shot a look toward Hannah. "Wait. We may have a problem."

"Why are you looking at me?" Hannah asked.

"It's a matter of paperwork. Insurance. The horse wouldn't be covered under my policy, because, technically, I don't own her."

Hannah looked at Shelton. "How valuable is your horse?"

"She's my best mare. You don't want to know."

Hannah huffed out a deep breath. "And how important is Tilly to the show?"

"Without her, or a suitable replacement, we'd have to cut at least half of the animal segments."

"So, this is a big deal," she surmised.

"Huge."

An idea occurred to her. "Shelton, can I speak to you for a moment?" Hannah motioned for Shelton to follow.

He looked confused, but he stepped off to the side with her.

"I have an idea. Sell Jazz your horse."

"Are you crazy? I'm not about to sell my horse!"

"Not for real," she hastily assured him. "Just make up a bill of sale that would pass scrutiny if, for some reason, God forbid, you had to make an insurance claim."

"God forbid is right!" he all but squeaked. "This is a prized piece of horseflesh we're talking about! She comes from a distinguished bloodline and has birthed three world champions."

"So, naturally, you want her fully insured, and Jazz would have to own her for that to happen. So, sell her the horse for the weekend."

Shelton continued to look skeptical. "You don't understand. That horse is like a part of my family. I'd just as soon saw off my right arm as lose that horse."

"You won't lose her. It would be on paper, only."

He was clearly torn. He thought about it for a long moment, but when Shelton finally looked back down into her face, his brown eyes were sad. "I'm sorry, Hannah. I'd do just about anything to help you. That's why I'm here this weekend, taking on a job I don't have time for. It was important to you, and I wanted to help you. But this. This is asking too much."

Hannah was disappointed, but she tried to understand his point of view.

"It's just that we don't know this woman," he continued, even though she said nothing more. "We don't know that we can trust her. What if she claims the sale is legit, and I lose my horse for real? I can't take that chance. Not even for you," he said sorrowfully.

"I understand," Hannah said softly. His love and devotion to his horse was admirable.

"If it was any other horse…" he said. "But not Ladybird. She's special."

"Don't give it another thought." To show there were no hard feelings, Hannah patted his arm before they returned to the others.

"So," Hannah announced. "I have a suggestion."

Shelton looked at her sharply, but she continued, "Let's use Shelton's horse, and she'll be covered under my insurance policy, should anything happen. Which, I'm sure, it won't. Will that work?"

"If you have a standard liability policy that covers people and animals while on your property."

"I do."

"Well," Jazz hesitated, looking skeptical. "It isn't ideal, but I suppose it's the best we can do. I'm sure that hunky lawyer of yours will point out that you purchased a policy from us. However, without me owning the horse, it clearly won't be included in that coverage. He may object." She rubbed her forehead, thinking aloud, "But if he's out of town until tonight…"

"Walker is just looking out for our best interests," Hannah defended him. "And right now, our best interest is to have a fully functioning show. If we have to cut half the show, we can't expect the audience to pay full price. And at half price, *none* of us would make any money," she reasoned.

"It's highly unusual," Jazz warned.

"Let me handle Walker. You handle the show."

"Are you sure?"

She had a moment of serious doubt. She considered calling Walker right now, to get his take on the situation. But he was in an important meeting, and she promised not to call except under dire circumstances. She didn't think this qualified as such, not when the solution was so simple.

"No. I'm not sure," she admitted, "but I don't see another way around the problem."

Jazz's bright smile returned. "Okay, then, let's do this!" She clapped her hands together excitedly, already making plans.

Shelton tugged on her hand, pulling her around for a hug. "Thank you, Hannah," he said sincerely, wrapping his long arms around her in a heartfelt hug.

"Thank *you*. You're the one providing the horse. Once again, you save the day!"

"I know this isn't the right time," he said, gazing down at her. "But when this is over, I plan to show you exactly how special I think you are."

Unsure how to respond, Hannah cleared her throat and gently extracted herself from his arms. "I have to get back to the inn. Good luck."

CHAPTER 12

Hannah arrived back at the inn as the first car pulled up. The doors of the green mini-van opened and three rumpled children spilled out, all speaking at once. From her vantage point inside, she couldn't tell if they were laughing or fighting, but one thing she knew for certain: they were loud. Not for the first time, she questioned her wisdom in career choices.

Taking her place behind the check-in counter, she argued with herself that it hadn't exactly been *her* choice. JoeJoe made the decision for her when he purchased the inn.

Her alter ego made the argument that while he had given the inn to her as a gift, it was her decision to accept it. It was her decision to stay. As Pierce pointed out less than an hour ago, her uncle was a very rich man. Whether she accepted the present made no impact on his portfolio. To him, it was merely a novelty, gifting his niece a town that bore her name. A story he could tell at dinner parties and among his millionaire friends.

No, staying had been her choice. Taking on the challenge of running the historic property was her decision. *Her* career choice.

At exactly two forty-seven, Hannah had the auspicious honor of checking in her very first guest. Del Hatfield's fateful overnight stay several weeks ago didn't count. This one was legitimate, and it was the first of what she hoped would be many more to come.

At the very least, there would be five more that evening, with still more the next day. All seven rooms in the inn were booked, and both cabins. The third cabin would be completed soon, just in time for the busy July Fourth weekend.

As the Elliott family tromped outside to the Anheim Cabin, escorted by the inn's exuberant Great Pyrenees, Hannah turned to Fred. "Now what do we do?"

"What do you mean, dear?"

"Is that it? We just hand them their key and leave them to it?"

"Pretty much," the older woman smiled. "This is *their* vacation, dear. We're a part of it, and yet we aren't."

Hannah propped her chin into her hands and sulked. "What a letdown. After all the excitement of watching them drive up, listening to the kids ask a hundred questions and recall every single thing they ever did here in the past, listening to Mrs. Elliott go on and on about the improvements we made, checking in my very first guest—without a single glitch, I might add—and the drumroll in my head as I handed over that first key, just sitting here now, doing nothing, is a bummer."

Fred patted her shoulder and laughed. "Hang on to that thought. I promise you, not all check-ins go this smoothly. And remember, the next several guests are staying in the house. You'll be amazed at how full—and loud—the inn will be once they all get here." She started to walk away, but turned to add, "Oh, and there's a reason

I suggested the Elliotts stay in the cabin. I, too, remember all the things those children did."

Hannah spent the next ten minutes feeling very innkeeper-ly. She checked the reservation book, congratulated herself on a successful first mission, and committed the names of their upcoming guests to memory.

She had this *nailed.*

Once all the guests checked in, she would go down to the show and nail phase two of opening night. Why had she been so worried? Things were zipping right along, just as planned.

Hannah grabbed a stack of brochures to carry into the inner office. She planned to take them with her tonight when she worked the gate, handing them out to prospective guests.

As she entered the office, a sound drew her attention. It was more of a guttural snort than an actual word. Hannah glanced up, saw the woman standing in the middle of the room, and promptly threw the brochures into the air. A cry of surprise squeaked from her, much like when she slipped on the lettuce.

The woman wore little more than rags. Layers upon layers of rags, from head to toe. Upon second glance, Hannah realized that some of the rags had fur. One boasted a long, shaggy tail. Another had a black pointed nose, narrow-set eyes, and sharp tips for ears. *Fox fur*, she thought with a cringe, its face still intact. She had the impression of feathers and beads, strips of leather, and coarsely woven cloth, although she couldn't say for certain. The image was blurred, as if projected onto the furnishings in the room.

This must be Gouyen, the Native American medicine woman. The elusive third ghost who inhabited the inn.

It was disconcerting enough, simply seeing a ghost. It didn't help that this one stood directly in Hannah's path, arms crossed, and feet planted in a determined stance. The expression on her leathery face was stoic, making it impossible to judge her friendliness.

Yet she had appeared before Hannah, so that had to account for something. Choosing to see it as a positive sign, Hannah gathered her courage and attempted to connect with the spirit. It took two tries of swallowing her fear before her voice came out. "Hello. I—I'm sorry I screamed. You startled me."

Another grunt.

Great conversation we have going. I babble, you grunt.

Biting on her lip, Hannah tried again. She touched a hand to her chest. "I'm Hannah."

The reply sounded nothing like a name. It sounded more like the poor woman was constipated.

"Can—Can I help you?"

In response, the ghost extended her arm toward Hannah. Hannah's first inclination was to shrink away, until she realized the woman seemed to be handing her something. Her fingers curled, as if holding an invisible object.

"I… don't understand," Hannah said.

The woman grunted again and shook her arm, insisting Hannah take the offering.

Far be it from me to insult a ghost. Legs trembling, Hannah took a few hesitant steps forward, reaching out and pretending to accept the unseen item. As her hand crossed the plane where Gouyen's image had been, the apparition faded.

"Hello?" Confused by her sudden disappearance, Hannah looked around the room. "Are you still here? Hello?"

Moments before, a distinct chill had penetrated the room. The temperature felt normal now, leading Hannah to believe the spirit was no longer present.

Oh, well. It could have gone worse, she decided.

She spotted something in the floor where Gouyen had stood. Retrieving it, she stared in surprise at the small leather pouch. It looked old and worn and was tied together with a thin string of rawhide. She turned the item over in her hands, wondering where it had come from. But when she lifted the pouch to her nose and sniffed, she knew exactly who had left it.

Gouyen. It held her scent.

At the time, Hannah hadn't consciously acknowledged the unique smell. There had been too many other things to process, her own fear being one of them. But one whiff of the pouch, and she realized she had smelled this same scent earlier. Subconsciously, a thought had flashed through her mind, wondering if she tracked in dirt on her feet. It wasn't an unpleasant odor, but it reminded Hannah of tromping through wet leaves and damp earth on a cloudy autumn day.

Had this been what Gouyen was trying to give her? She knew that only the most powerful of spirits were capable of moving physical objects, and that it took a great deal of energy to do so. Did Gouyen expend all her energy, leaving this gift for her? Was that why she faded so quickly?

And why, Hannah wondered, had she left her a gift in the first place? The stoic old spirit hadn't seemed the type for housewarming presents.

"Hannah?" Sadie said, passing by the office and seeing her there. "Why are there papers all over the floor? What's that in your hand?"

"I'm not sure." Hannah held the pouch out to her friend.

"Where did you get this?" Sadie asked, turning it over for closer inspection. "This looks like an old Indian medicine bag."

"Medicine bag?"

The older woman nodded. "Sometimes they held healing herbs, sometimes amulets to ward off evil spirits. See the tiny little beads sewn in? They're black, so I'd say this was meant to deflect evil." She handed the bag back, asking, "Do they sell these in the show? Because I can tell you, that's the best imitation I've ever seen. That almost looks authentic."

"It is authentic."

"What do you mean?"

Hannah took a deep breath, speaking through the sigh. "I think I just met Gouyen. She left this for me."

A gasp escaped the older woman. "You can't be serious! In all the years I've lived here, I've only seen her twice."

Hannah described the woman she had seen and their strange encounter.

"That definitely sounds like Gouyen," Sadie agreed. "But why would she feel the need to leave you a medicine bag, especially one to ward off evil spirits?"

"Maybe she wanted to wish me well?" Hannah suggested, her hopeful tone clearly fabricated. "Keep me safe from crazy guests?" They both knew she was reaching.

Sadie looked at her in silent reprimand. "I don't think this is a housewarming present, dear."

"I don't, either," Hannah admitted. A sense of dread lodged itself in her stomach. "Which can only mean one thing."

Sadie nodded in solemn agreement. "She's trying to protect you from the evil that's already present."

CHAPTER 13

Gates opened an hour and a half before the show. This allowed the crowd time to stroll through the carnival games, get in the spirit of the evening, and to indulge in their favorite treats and eats. As dusk moved in, strings of colorful lights and the twinkle of carnival tunes gave the evening a festive feel. The air was sweet and fragrant with the mingled aromas of popcorn, cotton candy, and *fried everything*, as Walker put it.

With all but one of the guests checked in at the inn—Sadie would stay behind to hold down the fort—Hannah was able to experience both opening day events to the fullest. After fulfilling hostess duties at the inn, she hurried to the show site, and was there to greet the first person through the turnstile.

"Holy boomtown, there's a lot of people already here!" she told Pierce, who manned the gates with her. "I didn't realize so many people would come out early for the carnival. I've tried counting, but I lost track with that last carload of teenagers."

"That's what the turnstile is for," he reminded her. "And you're definitely your uncle's niece. He's the only other person I've ever heard use that phrase."

"He made it up years ago. Don't make the mistake of asking him why," she suggested, with a look of mock horror. "It's a long and convoluted story."

"Hand me some of your brochures, and I'll pass them out, too," he offered.

Hannah turned to grab the extra stack from her bag. Out of the corner of her eye, she saw Guy and John Boy in a heated conversation.

"What's that about?" she asked, nodding toward the men. "They don't look very happy."

"Guy's a bit of a hothead. And John Boy likes to boss everyone around, so it's not a good combination."

"I imagine it's hard, being on the road so much, and living and working together in such close quarters. I imagine tempers can run high at times," Hannah commiserated.

"Guy didn't like them replacing Rusty with an outsider. He thought his brother would get the job."

"Surely, he realizes Shelton is only temporary."

"That's how I started out," Pierce said with a grin. "I was hired as a temporary two years ago, and I'm still here. Much to John Boy's dismay, I might add."

That could explain the other heated discussion she had witnessed, when the manager stalked off in anger. That was just prior to the heated kiss she saw.

"Holy boomtown, there's a lot going on around here," she muttered under her breath. Maybe she should get a scorecard to keep track of it all.

"You don't know the half of it." Pierce chuckled, obviously hearing her remark.

After greeting a family of four and two teenage girls who made googly eyes at Pierce, Hannah asked him to explain his comment.

"For starters, Daphne is John Boy's ex. John Boy is now involved with Talia, although they like to think no one knows, particularly Jazz and Petro. He's Talia's father, by the way, and roughly the same age as John Boy. Rusty couldn't stand Daphne, but Guy, his best friend and roommate, is crazy over her. That's what half their arguments were about. Daphne, however, keeps making passes at me, even though I keep telling her I'm not interested."

"Yeah, I think I may know where your interests lie," Hannah teased.

He made no comment as another family moved through the line. When time allowed, he offered a few more examples of the drama unfolding behind the scenes. Some of the stories were funny, some of them little more than idle gossip. As show time approached and the crowd grew heavier, there was no more time for small talk.

It appeared Hannah had worried for nothing. They had a sell-out crowd, well before the show started. She stayed at the gate to make pre-sales for the next day and to chat with the disappointed people she had to turn away, while Pierce disappeared to prep for his first skit.

As she closed the gates and tucked the moneybox into her bag for safekeeping, Hannah thought about some of the tales Pierce told. She wondered if John Boy was as domineering as he sounded, or if Pierce's account of the manager was jaded. It sounded to her like John Boy was particularly hard on Rusty. She couldn't help but feel sorry for the deceased man. With his boss and his so-called best friend always upset with him, it was no wonder he was so grumpy. In truth, it sounded like he didn't get along well with any of the crew.

Could any of them, she wondered, *have wanted him dead?* It was a silly thought, she knew. The sheriff's office had ruled it a natural death. There was no reason to borrow trouble and imagine his death to be something more than a heart attack. Obviously, the gift from Gouyen had her spooked. And who knew? Sadie's assumption that it was intended to ward off evil spirits might be completely off track.

But as her hand brushed against the small leather pouch nestled in her purse, a chill moved through Hannah's shoulders.

Sadie, she knew, was seldom wrong.

Hannah squeezed into a seat in the bleachers and settled in for the show. For the hundredth time, she wished that Walker was there beside her, but his text said he was delayed. There was the possibility he would stay overnight, but he promised to be home the next day.

Determined to enjoy the show, Hannah shared the crowd's excitement as the overhead lights dimmed and the spotlight moved to the stage in front of the 'town.' The first skit had the crowd roaring with laughter. The dog act was next, winning over the hearts of the audience and amusing them with the hound dog who thought he was a Dachshund. The pace slowed for Ted's mournful solo, but soon picked up again with the next comedy skit. Hannah was impressed with how smoothly the cast moved from one segment to the next.

Pierce Maldonado, she soon discovered, was an exceptional showman. He charmed the crowd with little more than his smile and a few witty lines. With Talia as his assistant, he asked for participation from the audience. Dozens of hands shot up from the engaged fans, but he finally chose two men from opposites sides of the stands. One was tall and thin, wearing shorts and sandals on the warm Texas evening. The other was shorter, wearing jeans and boots, not to mention a priest's collar with his black jacket.

They invited the men down to the stage and started their bit. Halfway through, a llama strutted across the
stage, interrupting their scene. All eyes turned to the llama and the man chasing it. "Petro" Petrosian was decked
out in full cowboy attire and a pair of very thick glasses,
shouting in heavily accented English about his 'horse'
that got away. Once again, the crowd roared at the hilarious antics of the actors.

When the near-sighted cowboy finally climbed into the saddle and rode his 'horse' off stage, Pierce and
Talia turned back to their guests. The tall man now wore a
pair of baggy jeans that struck well above his sandaled
feet, and the other man wore khaki shorts with his cowboy boots and priest collar. The audience ate it up, and
Hannah beamed with pride. Bringing *Hats Off* to town
had been a wise move on her part.

The gunfight took place just before the twenty-
minute intermission. When the stage turned to face the
rodeo arena, the second half of the show began. This half
was more about drawing oohs and ahhs than it was about
laughter. The crowd stayed thoroughly engaged, impressed with one daring feat after another. Even the barrel
racing had a twist; the contestants rode backwards, or
with their horses blindfolded. Daphne did a brilliant balancing act on the high wire, and Talia delighted the crowd
with her blazing batons.

Two lighthearted routines broke the tension of the
second half of the show. Kids from the stands came down
to herd and rope the fluffy sheep running willy-nilly
around the pen. The crowd loved the playful interaction
between them, and all participants won ribbons and extra
tokens for the carnival games.

The other routine involved a chuck wagon race.
After an exaggerated bet between the participants, three
wagons raced around the perimeter. When the dust
cleared and the winner announced, even Hannah won-

dered when and how the drivers had switched wagons. The audience was still chuckling when the final act began, but as Jazz rode out into the arena, a hush fell upon the crowd. She wore a dazzling outfit that twinkled in the spotlight, assuring that all eyes were upon her as she went through her paces.

There was no doubt she was a skilled rider. She made even the most difficult tricks look easy. She stood atop the horse's back and danced a jig, as the steed carried her out of the ring and Pierce took her place in the spotlight. While he did his own series of impressive stunts, Hannah swore she could hear women swooning in the stands.

But the real magic happened when Jazz returned to the arena and they performed their stunts as a duet. Jazz was dressed all in white. Pierce wore all black. She was dainty and elegant. He was strong and graceful. Together, they were the perfect pair. It was like a ballet on horseback, and by the time the spotlight dimmed and the music faded, the crowd was on their feet.

Hannah cheered as loudly as the people around her did. The show was brilliant. Her heart thudded in excitement, and dollar signs swam before her eyes. After tonight's performance, she had no doubt that the rest of the weekend would be a sell-out.

She only wished Walker were there with her to celebrate.

Hannah wanted to stay and congratulate Jazz for a job brilliantly done, but she had been gone from the inn long enough. She slipped through the crowd and made her way out the gate, noting all the smiling faces and enthusiastic responses around her. The majority of the people headed to the carnival games to try their hand at luck, or to the food trucks to sample their favorite treat. Per their agreement, *Hats Off* kept all proceeds from the trailers. If they met a certain threshold, they applied a percentage of sales toward the booking fee. There was no way to monitor sales from the trailers—unlike at the gate, where the turnstile kept an accurate count—but Hannah had no reason to believe that *Hats Off* would be anything less than honest. So far, she was wonderfully impressed.

She gave Sadie a complete recap of the show as she helped prep for tomorrow morning's breakfast buffet.

"It was that good, was it?" The older woman smiled, noting how Hannah's face still glowed.

"It was wonderful! And you should have seen Jazz and Pierce do the final number. It gave me chills watching it."

"Did Fred get to see it?" Sadie wanted to know. She placed empty chaffing dishes on the antique sideboard. In the morning, all she had to do was fill them with deliciousness.

The door opened and her sister glided in, her arms spread wide. Stars still sparkled in her eyes. "Did I ever! It was magnificent!" She twirled around on the toe of red leather boots. "It makes me want to get back on a horse and do my old routine again."

"Don't be foolish!" Sadie chided. "At your age, you'd break every bone in your body when you fell!"

"Who said I would fall? I, my dear, am a professional." She twirled and glided, imagining herself on the back of a horse.

"Fifty years ago, you were a professional. Now, you're just old."

"You don't have to be mean about it," Fred snapped, stopping mid-glide.

"Not mean, just realistic. Make yourself useful and put out the plates."

Without another word about reviving her former glory, Fred pulled a stack of dishes from the cupboard below and divided them into two stacks.

"You're all set for tomorrow, right, Fred?" Hannah asked. "I've never been in a trail ride before, much less hosted one. I wouldn't have the first clue of what to do."

"Don't worry. I've been in more than my share. This is just a mini version of the real thing. No overnight camping, no chuck wagon. A pale comparison to the real deal, but it makes the guests happy. And this year, there's the added bonus of having the show in our backyard. We'll end the ride there."

"Jazz had a great idea, letting us ride in the parade through the middle of their 'town.' I can't wait to surprise the riders. And the audience, too!"

"We call it a grand entry, dear," Fred gently corrected her. "You'll ride in it, won't you?" Fred asked.

Hannah looked uncertain. "I think I should probably stay here at the inn."

"Nonsense!" Sadie said. "I can handle anything that comes up. This is your shining moment, girl. You should ride in the grand entry, even if you don't do the trail ride."

"I'm definitely not doing the trail ride!" She laughed at the notion of such. "But are you sure, Sadie? Wouldn't you like to go to the performance, and let me stay here at the inn?"

"Don't worry about me. I'll catch the five o'clock show."

She turned back toward Fred. "Will there be a horse for me to ride? I know Walker loaned us some for the guests, but all of them are booked."

"I'm sure he has more. And if he doesn't, you could always ask Shelton Long to bring you one."

Since they brought the subject up…

"What do you know about Shelton?" Hannah asked, hoping to sound nonchalant. She didn't want to encourage their fondness for matchmaking. For neither having ever married, the sisters were hopeless romantics.

"Not much, to be honest," Sadie said with a frown. "He hasn't lived here very long. Two years or—"

"—maybe three," from Fred.

"I believe he came here from East Texas."

"I know he's good with horses."

Sadie snorted. "Sister swears you can judge a man by the way he treats his horse, but I'm not so sure about that."

"Well," Hannah interjected, "I do know that Shelton is crazy about his horse. He has one, Ladybird, that he says is like family."

"Mark my words," Fred said. "A man who treats his horse right treats his woman right, too."

Hannah scowled. "Who said anything about being Shelton Long's woman? Just because he kissed me—"

"He kissed you? When?" Sadie demanded.

"Uhm, the other day. The day I introduced him to Jazz."

"I had no idea," Fred said. "In fact, I thought I saw something between him and Jazz. They looked so cozy together when I saw them talking tonight." She clicked her tongue, disappointed in herself for misreading the situation.

"Does Walker know?" Sadie quizzed.

"Of course not! Not," Hannah sniffed, "that it's any of his business."

"The two of *you* looked rather cozy this morning, when he brought you those flowers." Sadie was firmly entrenched in Camp Walker.

"I was asking about Shelton," she reminded the sisters. "Why doesn't Walker like him?"

"You'd have to ask him about that, dear."

"I did. He's very evasive, but I think it must have something to do with a lawsuit."

"Hmm, you may be right," Sadie said thoughtfully. "I seem to recall something about one of Bert Hiel's horses. Something about—"

"—his horse being shod with the wrong size shoe," Fred recalled. "I remember it now. Shelton claimed the shoes were sized wrong by the manufacturer, but Bert said it did permanent damage to his best horse."

"That can happen?"

Fred's gray head bobbed as she explained, "You fit the shoe to the hoof, not the hoof to the shoe. If you put too small of a shoe on a horse—say, an ought, instead of a size one—and trim the hoof to fit, you may trim it too far and cause the horse to go lame."

"And Walker represented Bert, I suppose." Hannah surmised. "Who won?"

"I think it's still an open case."

"Which is why Walker won't talk about it. He's a true professional, you know," Sadie beamed.

"Does Shelton have family here?"

"Just his horse," Sadie quipped.

"No family that I know of," said Fred. "Come to think of it, to be so friendly, he doesn't talk about himself very much."

"He asked me out, but I'm not sure I want to go." Hannah had no qualms about confiding in the sisters. They had become more than her best friends. They were like the mother she never had. Jacqueline Duncan had always been more concerned about being a star than being a confidante to her daughter.

"Why not?" Fred wanted to know.

Ignoring her sister's input, Sadie nodded. "I think that's for the best."

Hannah answered with, "I'm not looking for romance right now."

"I agree with you, dear. Not about the romance, but about Shelton Long. Sure, he's easy on the eye, and who doesn't appreciate those long legs of his? But Walker's legs are almost as long, and he's even better looking." Sadie closed her eyes with a dreamy look upon her face. "I always did favor dark looks over blond."

"This isn't your love life we're talking about," Fred reminded her sister. "And I'm just as fond of Walker as you are. All I'm saying is that Shelton Long is good with animals. And in my book, that says something about a man."

CHAPTER 14

They met back at the trailer, long after the sounds of the evening had died away. The gates were closed, the trucks shuttered, the lights all out.

It had been a successful first day, but tomorrow promised to be even better. Saturdays were always good, because they could squeeze in three shows. That meant three times the opportunity to scam unsuspecting guests. Three times the ways to find creative cash flow and those *special sponsorships* that kept their operation running.

"How did we do?"

"Not bad. Collected three credit card numbers. Lifted about a hundred and fifty dollars in cash. Not a lot, but not bad for a one-horse town."

"Three cards? I warned you not to get greedy!"

"Relax. That dude in the black jacket had at least three platinum cards in his wallet. Most likely, he'll never notice when one or two of them are used. Next year, in a town far, far away."

"That *dude* was a priest."

"God bless him." This, with a mocking smile and the sign of the cross. "He doesn't know it, but he made a very generous donation to our cause."

"I hope you were smart about taking the cash."

Another smart grin. "The craziest thing happened. A money clip fell out of the one man's shorts when he swapped clothes. The outer bills stayed in place, but would you believe the middle bills came loose?"

"Good. That's the way to do it. My old man is a master at the art of *lightening* a person's pocket. He says the trick is to always leave change."

"Change?"

"People notice when anything larger than a twenty is missing. Instead of just swiping a bill, he likes to swap it for a couple of ones. If it was a fifty or a hundred, he leaves a ten and a few small bills."

"But that's stupid. Why give back part of your hit?"

"Not stupid. Brilliant. People assume they broke the bill and just don't remember it. Why would they suspect they'd been robbed, if they have change?"

The disapproving frown lifted into an impressed smile. "You're right. Brilliant."

"Yep. I learned the art of the scam from my old man. He's the best."

"I just hope that brother of yours doesn't stir up too much trouble. We were doing just fine on our own. We don't need him butting in."

"Lucky for us, he, too, was taught by the best."

CHAPTER 15

The breakfast buffet was not only delicious, but also crowded. As the sisters predicted, several local people showed up for the event, touting reservations. Hannah still didn't appreciate being left in the dark about the buffet, but she couldn't fault its success. She supposed after all these years, the Tanner women knew exactly what they were doing.

She helped Sadie clean the kitchen as the guests dispersed for the day. Some had plans for sightseeing, some for strolling through the shops of nearby Fredericksburg, and several were riding in the trail ride. Hannah saw the maiden voyage off, thankful that Walker had returned in time to help with the event. She knew nothing about tightening cinches or adjusting bits or properly distributing weight atop a horse's back. Best to leave those details to the experts, Walker and Fred.

Hannah was at her desk, handling paperwork details, as the Sanchez family came down from their room. The son ran ahead, eager to start his day of fun and excitement, while his parents descended at a more leisurely pace.

"That boy!" his mother laughed, with a shake of her head. "I wish I had half his energy!"

"He's just excited, Mom." Hannah made excuses for the child with an indulgent smile. "Was everything okay with your room? Can we do anything while you're out?"

"No, no, everything is perfect. That little pull-out couch is just right for Eli Junior. He especially liked the toy spurs y'all left on the table. He's wearing them now."

Hannah tilted her head in confusion. "Spurs?"

"That was such a cute touch, especially since we're in the Vaquero Room. Do you always do that for the kids, or is it because the Wild West show is in town? We went to last night's performance, by the way. It. Was. Fabulous."

Hannah was glad that Anita Sanchez rattled on about the show, because she had no ready answer about the toy spurs. Was that another detail Sadie and Fred had forgotten to mention?

Thanks to another of the quirky stipulations in Miss Wilhelmina's will, Hannah had received a large bonus to remodel and update the inn. One of the first orders of business was to give each of the seven rooms a theme. The Vaquero Room was dedicated to Orlan Varela, himself, and decorated accordingly. Hannah had personally chosen the Spanish-inspired furnishings and décor. She had even added special touches like *reatas* wound around lighting fixtures, Mexican horse blankets as window treatments, and had created a sombrero medallion for the ceiling fan. But this was the first she heard of toy spurs.

"Momma, Momma!" Little Eli ran up to tug on his mother's hand. "Come see my friend! He has spurs, just like mine! And he has a *gun*!" The boy's eyes were alight with excitement.

"A gun?" cried his mother.

"Probably one of the actors from last night's show," Eli Senior assured his wife, but his laughter sounded nervous. "Right?" He looked at Hannah for confirmation.

The child had come from the lounge area. Hannah spotted Orlan Varela beside the great stone fireplace, a huge smile upon his face. The ghost waved in their direction, and to her surprise, young Eli returned the gesture.

"Isn't he cool?"

"Who? I don't see anyone," his father said, craning his neck to see the person who held his son's fascination.

"That man right there, by the fireplace. He looks just like the man in our room."

"What man in our room, honey?" his mother asked.

"The one that gave me the spurs. The one in the painting."

"Eli," his mother said, getting that matronly tone of warning in her voice. "We've talked about this. I appreciate that you have a vivid imagination, but you can't be making up tales. People in paintings cannot come to life and give you presents." She shot Hannah an apologetic look. "We had a long conversation about this last night. After an hour, I thought we had convinced him."

The look Hannah slipped the spirit wasn't apologetic. It was downright accusatory. In response, Orlan offered a sheepish grin and a shrug.

Who knew the ghost had a soft spot for children?

Thinking it best to change the subject, Hannah asked where the family headed for the day.

"We heard something about a huge rock people like to climb? It sounds like a good way to expend some of this boy's energy!"

"Yes, the Enchanted Rock State Natural Area," Hannah said. "About thirty minutes north of here. It's a huge dome of pink granite—the second biggest rock in the United States—with an elevation of 1800 feet at the summit. Here, let's get you a brochure."

By the time the Sanchez family was gone, so was Orlan Varela. Hannah made a mental note to talk to the spirit about his antics the next time she saw him. *Was there a way to summon him*, she wondered. She knew so little about the spirit world. She really needed to educate herself on the matter. It would go on list three, the *Critical Things to Do When I Have Time* list.

Before she could settle into her chair, the front door opened again.

"Knock, knock," said the blond man.

"Good morning, Shelton," Hannah smiled. "How are you this morning?"

"Busier than a one-winged momma hen with a brood of chicks," he grinned. He used his exaggerated Southern drawl, the one he knew was sappy but endearing.

"That bad, huh?" she smiled.

"Good, actually," he corrected, taking off his cowboy hat as he sauntered across the great room. "When you're working, busy is always good. Keeps the money rollin' in."

"I didn't get a chance to tell you last night, but the show was excellent."

"Shoot, I didn't have much to do with it," he denied modestly. "Just opened gates and handed reins to the riders. The crew works together like a well-oiled machine. I just had to squeeze the can from time to time."

"I'm sure you had a bigger part than just that. By the way, which horse was Ladybird?"

"The pretty little dapple mare," he replied.

Hannah didn't remember seeing a dapple, but that was hardly surprising. The show had so many amazing elements, it was difficult to absorb them all, much less remember them the next day. She looked forward to seeing the show again today. And this time, she would keep her eyes open for the mare.

"Speaking of Ladybird, that's why I'm here. I'd be honored if you rode her today in the grand entry."

Knowing how much he cared about his horse, Hannah was flattered, but hesitant. "Oh, I don't know about that. I—I'm not even certain I'll participate."

"But you have to," the lanky man encouraged. "You're the one who brought the show to Gillespie County. After last night's success, you gotta know how popular that makes you! The people will expect no less."

"Oh, but—"

"No buts. I've already gotten Ladybird all spiffed up for it. Teased her tail, gave her some glitter highlights, the works. All she needs is the prettiest little lady in three counties to ride her in." He winked at her, bringing a blush to her cheeks. "And before you ask, there's no need to fret over what to wear. I spotted something in wardrobe that will be perfect for you."

In the end, Hannah agreed to ride the mare. Which was why, an hour later, Hannah was dressed in the most ridiculous outfit she had ever worn in her life, preparing to mount a horse that was bigger than any mare she had ever ridden.

With white jeans so tight they could have been painted onto her skin, she wondered how she would lift her leg to crawl into the saddle. If the buttons on the low-cut blouse should fail, she would give the audience more than a casual peek. Even Hannah was impressed with the amount of cleavage all but popping from the too-tight blouse, but she felt ridiculous in the sequined red and blue creation, especially with the ten-inch-long white fringe beneath the arms. If she flapped her arms while at a gallop, she wondered if she might fly.

As she contemplated the best way to maneuver the tight pants and the saddle horn, Shelton appeared. "Need help?" he grinned.

She pursed her lips. "It may be easier to parachute down and land astraddle."

He laughed at her exaggeration. "That's where being so tall comes in handy," he said. Before she could suspect his intent, he stepped onto the nearby platform, scooped her up in his arms, and deposited her into the saddle.

"There. All done."

"Wait! Wh—!" By the time she formed a proper protest, she was sitting atop the horse. She grabbed onto the saddle horn and laughed nervously. "Why did you do that?"

"Looked to me like you needed help, and I aim to please, ma'am." He tipped the brim of his hat, his face split in an amused grin.

"Ohmygosh, I can't believe you did that!" She was still breathless. She took a few moments to still her pounding heart and to get her bearings. She hesitantly touched the rim of the saddle, and the reins, and the back of the horse's neck, like a person getting into an unfamiliar automobile and checking out the instrument panel.

"It's all there," Shelton teased. He grabbed the bridle and pulled the horse's neck around toward her. "Say hello to Ladybird. Lady, this here is the special gal I was telling you about."

He made the introductions as if we were introducing two people. Hannah laughed, all the while wondering just how far he took his affection for the horse. *Obsessed much?*

"This," she told him, "is the biggest mare I've ever seen. Or ridden. Are you sure I can handle her?" She felt the strength of the horse beneath her, giving new meaning to the term *horsepower.*

"Ladybird? Aw, she's just a big ole' baby!" Shelton laughed at the suggestion. He nuzzled the horse's face with his own, his voice taking on a surprisingly gentle tone. "Aren't you, girl? That's right, just my big ole' baby girl."

Hannah could have sworn the horse kissed him. The dapple snuggled her velvety nostrils against his cheek and parted her lips, giving a soft nicker. Shelton laughed in delight, dropping a kiss onto the horse's long nose.

"Would you two like to be alone?" Hannah teased.

"Looks like we're making her jealous, girl," he told the horse. He pretended to whisper in her ear, but he said the words deliberately loud. "I'll meet you behind the stables at midnight." Patting the horse's neck affectionately, he released the bridle. When she shook her head and stomped, Hannah felt the quake rattle in her own shoulders.

"Seriously, this is a powerful horse!" Fear leaked into her voice.

"I told you, she's the mother of champions. That means mating with some powerful stallions. Not exactly a job for lightweights."

"What if I can't handle her?" Hannah worried.

"Relax. She's a highly trained animal. She knows exactly what to do."

Hannah still looked skeptical, but there was no time to protest. Jazz called for the riders to line up. When Shelton gently slapped Ladybird on the rump and said, "Take care of my girl," she wondered if he were talking to her or the mare. But as the steed began to move, she forgot about the farrier and concentrated on the horse. Namely, on staying in the saddle and not falling beneath the powerful legs carrying her ever closer to the crowd.

The plan was simple. As John Boy welcomed the crowd and introduced the show and their special grand entry participants, the National Anthem would begin. Hannah would lead the string of riders along the string of fake storefronts. Then she would turn and ride closer to the grandstands. Taking cues from the crew, she would set the pace so that a double line formed and they passed one another. Two such circles, Jazz said, was ample time to play the anthem, give the beaming trail riders maximum exposure to the fans in the stands, and to build anticipation for the show to come.

After the first round, Hannah relaxed. The horse was powerful, but well disciplined. She suspected the mare would have much preferred a faster pace, but she responded to Hannah's commands and kept her steps smooth and measured.

It happened as they turned for the home stretch. Hannah knew that in a typical grand entry, this was when the horses broke into a run, signifying the real show was about to begin. But Jazz had explained that they would keep to their slow and steady pace, allowing for the varied skill levels of the trail riders. Many, she knew, were sitting on a horse for the first time. For their safety, the retreat would be slow and orderly.

Ladybird, however, was trained for the spotlight. She knew the drill. She knew that if she raced for the exit, the crowd would cheer. Knew their excitement would fuel her energy and give her incentive to not simply perform, but to excel. Ladybird was a horse trained to please.

As the horse lunged forward, the sudden motion took Hannah by surprise. She grabbed for the saddle horn and held on for dear life, forgetting about the reins. Her body whipped forward, unsteady and wobbly over the neck of the horse.

Ladybird misinterpreted her rider's command. She took it as the signal to run faster. Responding to the cue, the horse's powerful hooves gobbled up more ground.

Hannah belatedly thought to jerk the reins. The horse abruptly shot to the right, toward the string of make-believe buildings. She barely missed the staged area, but her hooves clipped a guy-line. She kicked her hind legs to get the entanglement off her feet, launching herself—and her rider—into a hard pitch forward. By the grace of God, Hannah managed to stay in the saddle, but she heard fabric rip and something crash behind them. As the horse's feet slapped the ground, Hannah's teeth rattled in her head and the sunny overhead sky suddenly lit with stars.

The crowd thought it was part of the show. They roared in excitement, cheering on the fabulous exhibition ride. Wanting more, they were disappointed when the duo didn't turn back and preen for applause. Instead, the dapple raced away, carrying her rider with her.

Unsure of how to proceed without their leader, the other riders stopped in the tracks.

Only one horse thundered along the path behind the dapple. Riding in the rear of the line, Walker was at the far end of the street when he realized Hannah was in trouble. He ignored the cries of the crowd, who again thought it was part of the show. Dodging the confused trail riders, Walker paid no heed to the crewmembers stepping out and waving their arms, trying to slow him down. He leaned low over the neck of his stallion and slapped the reins, urging the steed to run faster. Like a cowboy in the movies, Walker rode hard and fast to rescue the damsel in distress.

The crowd loved it. They were on their feet, screaming at the top of their lungs in excitement. John Boy tried to keep up with the turn of events, offering a play-by-play of the action. From his lofty location near the high wire, he could still see the horses, even when the audience couldn't. Jazz practically shoved a young man off his horse and launched herself into the saddle, but not before glancing up at the crowd gone wild. She should consider working this scenario into the show. Not bothering with a horse, Shelton's long legs gobbled up territory as he did a fine job of keeping pace with Jazz and her horse. Somewhere along the way, she offered him a hand and he swung onto the horse behind her, never losing a beat.

Ahead of them, Walker caught up with Ladybird, his powerful stallion overtaking the well-matched mare. By the time he reached her, Hannah was barely hanging on. Her face was ashen, her dark hair was wild, and the white fringe on her shirt flew in all directions as one of her arms flapped haphazardly in the wind.

"Hang on, Hannah!" Walker yelled. "I've got you!"

He nudged his horse against the mare, not enough to knock her over, but with enough force to slow her down. The dapple gradually began to slow, but her hooves still thundered against the earth. If Hannah fell now, she would be trampled beneath one, or both horses.

"When I grab you," Walker yelled, his voice carrying over the sound of the hooves, the wind, and the crowd still roaring behind then, "turn loose of the horn. Got it?"

"Wh—What?" She turned her head to look at him, the shock evident in her face.

Walker leaned far out of the saddle and snaked his arm around her waist. "Turn loose, Hannah!" he said, feeling her resistance. At this pace, they would both be jerked from their saddles and trampled to death. "Turn loose. Now!"

Hannah did as he demanded. She screamed as she left the saddle. Any moment now, she would feel the sharp sting of steel as the horseshoes ripped through her flesh. Lose consciousness as eight muscled legs pounded her into the ground. With any luck, her foot wouldn't hang in the stirrup, and she wouldn't be dragged across the pasture. Any moment now, her world would go black, and Walker's face would be the last thing she would ever see.

She could think of worse things.

And then she realized she had *time* to think of those things. It took a full moment before she realized she wasn't being trampled to death. She *hadn't* fallen from the saddle. Walker had lifted her from her horse and slung her, none too gracefully, across his own saddle. Face down, no less. The saddle horn bit into her stomach as the horses slowed.

"Hannah!"

She heard the panic in Walker's voice. Glanced up to see the worry in his face. Saw the fear and the sheer relief of having her safe, and more or less in his arms. She struggled to sit up, twisting and squirming until she was in an upright position. She was half sidesaddle, half in Walker's lap, sitting backwards on the horse. She didn't care, because it allowed her to throw her arms around his waist and squeeze him so tightly he yelped.

"Are you okay?" he demanded.

"Yes!" She said the word in amazement, truly shocked to discover it was true. She had somehow managed to not only live through the horrific ride, but to come out of it in one piece. Her body was already sore, her head and her heart pounded at a dangerous tempo, and she tasted blood on her tongue. But she was alive!

Without thinking it through, Hannah released Walker's waist, grabbed his face in both her hands, and pressed a hard, fast kiss onto his lips. *She was alive!*

Jazz's borrowed horse slid to a stop behind them.

"Are you okay?" the show producer asked sharply.

"Hannah!" Shelton shrieked, sliding off the horse to hurry to her side. He looked up at the rumbled couple in concern, his sides heaving as he swallowed deep gulps of air. After his race across the pasture—first on foot, then bareback across the rump of a horse—he was painfully out of breath. It took him a moment to focus and form a coherent thought.

Hannah's blouse was ripped and gaping open, revealing far more than just cleavage. Her hair was wild and her face was pale, but flushed. Blood dribbled from the side of her mouth. When his eyes trailed to Walker, he saw a similar smudge of red around his mouth.

Then his eyes moved beyond the couple, to the horse lying on its side beyond them. "Lady!" he shrieked. He ran to the mare, falling onto his knees beside the animal. "What did you do to my horse!" he demanded, his hands traveling over her in a frantic pace.

The horse nickered and tucked her head into the crook of the tall man's shoulder. As Shelton crooned in concern and ran his hand lovingly over the horse, Walker looked down at Hannah. With the immediate danger passed, his stormy blue eyes managed a light of humor.

"They need to get a room," he murmured.

Hannah giggled. It was nerves, she was sure, but the giggle turned into a snicker. Before she could help it, she was laughing. The sound was contagious, begging Walker to join in.

Shelton Long was not amused. "What is wrong with you!" he screamed, looking back at them with contempt in his eyes. "This horse is injured, and all you can do is sit there laughing! Half naked, too, and kissing another man! Two days ago, you were kissing me!" he reminded her coldly.

Hannah and Walker looked down at the same time, both only now realizing the state of her undress. With a gasp, Hannah looked up, catching the look in his dark gaze. There was no doubt she saw appreciation there. Perhaps a touch of lust.

Both paled in comparison to the hurt she saw in his eyes. At the mention of her kiss with Shelton, the light in his blue gaze died, replaced by the look of thunder. She started to explain, but he wanted no explanation. Not from her.

"Don't you dare look at her," Walker demanded. His voice was as cold as an Arctic winter. Even as he spoke, he jerked his starched western shirt off, popping a button or two in his haste. He wrapped it around Hannah and pointed an angry finger at the man still kneeling beside his horse.

"I'm sorry if the horse is hurt, but you didn't even ask about Hannah. You care more about that mare than you do about her," he accused.

"I can see she's fine," Shelton shot back. "I can't say the same about the horse!"

As the farrier turned back to his beloved animal, Jazz turned in the saddle and waved at the crowd in the distance. She pumped her hands high, letting them know all was fine. The faint sound of their cheers wafted across the field. Despite the drama unfolding in the field, and despite the men's angry exchange, her message was clear. The show must go on.

Tucking the borrowed shirt more tightly around her, Hannah had to appreciate the way Walker stood up for her. Best of all, his manner was more protective than it was proprietary. The last thing she wanted was to become a coveted possession between the two men.

Not that she needed a man to speak for her, but at the moment, it was much appreciated. With each passing moment, she was slowly succumbing to the aftershock of the danger.

Walker felt her tremble. As Shelton helped his horse to her feet and worried over the way Ladybird favored her hind leg, Walker gently helped Hannah turn around, so that she sat correctly in the saddle. Pulling her back against his bare chest, he wrapped his arms around her and picked up the reins. Without as much as a glance to the other man and his limping horse, Walker heeled his steed in the flanks and swiftly carried Hannah back to the inn.

He avoided the area around the grandstands. The audience had already forgotten about them and was now enthralled with the opening skit. Walker held her with his arm tight against her waist, and Hannah clung to him with both hands. Neither spoke as they raced across the pasture and took a back way home, through the woods, and past the Tanner cabin. He reined in at the back door of the inn, slipping off the horse and holding his arms out to help her down, before Hannah even had time to think of how to get off in her skin-tight jeans.

Walker ushered her in the back door and into the nearby back office, shuttering them inside. She was in no shape to face guests, but that didn't stop Sadie. She followed them into the office.

"What happened to you!" Sadie cried.

"The horse. Grand entry. B—B—Bucked." Hannah managed the explanation in fragments.

"Are you all right? What are you doing in those skin-tight jeans and Walker's shirt?" Sadie asked, clucking around her like a mother hen. She had Hannah seated on the sofa, wrapped in an afghan, boots off, and with her feet propped up on a pillow, by the time she asked the next question. "Is that blood on your mouth? And on Walker's, too? How in the world—" She stopped mid-sentence, as the significance of the smear became evident. Biting back a pleased smile, she hovered over the disheveled woman. "Can I get you something? Water? Tea? Whiskey?"

The door burst open and Fred rushed into the room, clearly out of breath and flustered. "Oh, thank God you're all right!" she said, clutching her hand to her chest. "I saw the whole thing. I've never been so scared in all my life!"

"What exactly happened?" Sadie asked.

Fred was the one to tell the story. By then, Walker had plopped down on the couch near Hannah, close enough for emotional support. Not quite close enough for physical comforting. Sadie shoved a glass of sweet tea into Hannah's hands and rubbed her feet, even though that wasn't the part of her that hurt the worst.

Fred's rendition of events was quite colorful, painting a vivid scene of how things played out from her vantage point. When she reached the part where the horses raced into the field, out of sight, she nudged Walker to take over the story.

His version was short and to the point. "I caught up with her, pulled her onto my horse, and the only thing that sorry Shelton Long cared about was the danged mare!"

"That's it?" Fred stared at him in disbelief. "That's all you got?"

"What more do you want?" he glowered.

"The part where she's wearing your shirt and you're wearing her blood might be nice," the older woman said dryly.

In answer, Hannah dropped the blanket and opened the front of her borrowed shirt, careful to keep the view from Walker. Although in retrospect, it might be too late for that. He had already gotten an eyeful.

"Oh, my," Sadie said, a smile hovering on her lips.

"To his credit," Hannah said, "Shelton didn't stare. As Walker pointed out, he was much more concerned with his horse than he was with me." Remembering the way they had laughed at Walker's comment about getting a room, a smile tugged at her lips. When she glanced at the attorney, he knew exactly what she was thinking. They both burst out laughing. Again.

"Sister, I think I hear someone at the desk," Sadie said abruptly. "And I need to check on a pie I have in the oven."

"But I don't hear—Oh, yes. Yes, I do believe you're right."

Their hasty exit was quite obvious. Walker cocked an amused eyebrow before dropping his dark head back against the couch and hefting out a long sigh.

"What a day," he said. "And it's not even mid-afternoon yet."

"I hope I can move tomorrow," Hannah fretted. She pulled her feet off the ottoman, amazed she could bend her legs. Either the white pants had loosened, or the ordeal had scared ten pounds off her. She gingerly shifted on her bottom, trying not to wince.

"I recommend a long soak in a hot tub," he told her.

Several inches separated them on the sofa. Hannah reached out to cover his hand where it lay between them.

"Thank you, Walker, for coming to my rescue." Her voice was soft.

"Anytime, ma'am," he drawled, looking every bit the cowboy as he pretended to tip the hat he no longer wore. No doubt, he had lost it somewhere in his mad dash to save her. Hannah idly wondered how expensive it had been, or if he'd be able to salvage it. She tried not to think about how handsome he looked, sitting there in nothing but his jeans and boots.

"I'm serious. I don't know what I would have done if you hadn't—"

He silenced her by curling his fingers over hers, and reminding her gently, "But I did."

"Yes." Her smile was unsteady. "You did."

After a moment of silence, Hannah addressed the elephant in the room. "About what Shelton said…"

"Hannah, you don't have to say anything. You have the right to kiss whoever you please."

"I know." She leaned over to touch the smear of her blood, still on his chin. "And I did."

She heard the sharp intake of his breath. "Hannah—" His voice sounded pained.

"I know, I know," she said, holding her hands up in a gesture of surrender. "I know what you're going to say. You're going to say that you're my lawyer, and I'm your client, and that we can never be more than friends. Yada, yada, yada. But I just want you to know, *he* kissed me. I was a bit hysterical, and apparently, it was the fastest way to shut me up."

To her surprise, his dark eyes twinkled. "I may have to keep that in mind," he mused. Then his eyes darkened, their expression growing serious. "But that wasn't what I was going to say," he told her.

"It wasn't?"

"No. I was going to say that as much as I enjoy the view—" his eyes dropped to the front of his shirt, completely forgotten and hanging wide open, "—you may want to pull that shirt together."

With a furious blush, Hannah gasped and yanked the dual shirts closed over her exposed skin. When she jumped to her feet, she gasped for another reason. She was raw in places she forgot even existed.

"Hot bath," she moaned. "I definitely need a hot bath."

CHAPTER 16

Peeling off the skin-tight jeans and what remained of the sequined top, Hannah eased into the tub. She had the water as hot as her tender skin could tolerate. Her current paperback and a half-empty glass of wine perched on the edge of the tub. Notes of lavender and eucalyptus mingled with the tang of Epsom salts. It was three o'clock in the afternoon, but she pulled out all the stops, in a valiant effort to coax away her aches and pains.

Eyes closed, she heard a faint rustling noise in the room. She gave it no thought, until a new scent rode on the air. When the smell of damp earth hit her, her eyes popped open.

She let out another squeal of surprise. Without thinking, she sank down in the tub, until even her head buried beneath the water. Quite ineffective, it turned out, considering there were no bubbles to distort the image of her naked body in the clear bath. As she sputtered and surfaced, Hannah wondered if ghosts could see through bubbles, had she used any. What if they had x-ray vision?

Gouyen glared at her with her customary expression of *nothing*.

"I did it again, didn't I?" Hannah murmured, resisting the urge to cover her chest. Considering the day's events, and not knowing how long the spirit had been there, it seemed a bit useless. "I squealed. I'm sorry. I just never expected you here. In my bathroom." She was also babbling again, but the woman made her nervous. She was a *ghost*, for crying out loud. And she had a way of just staring…

The old woman grunted, in a sequence that Hannah assumed were words.

"I'm sorry. I don't speak your language."

Ghost or Indian. Take your pick. Oh, wait. We aren't supposed to say Indian anymore. It's politically incorrect. I should say I don't speak Native American.

Great! She was even babbling in her thoughts now.

In a rough, rusty voice, the spirit spoke again. It took a few moments for Hannah to realize she actually knew what she said.

"Warned you," the old woman croaked.

Hannah blinked in surprise. "Yes," she finally thought to say. "Yes, you did." She bobbed her head like one of those dolls people stuck on their car dash. Her likeness would have oversized blue eyes and long, dark hair. And a giant question mark splashed across its forehead. "But… what were you warning me about?"

"Evil."

"Evil. Got it."

Babbling! The warning dinged in her head.

"If you don't mind me asking, Gouyen, ma'am… Mrs. …er, Miss." Who knew how Native American medicine women were addressed, two centuries past? "Dr.? Oh, never mind. Can you just tell me where the evil is coming from?"

Her expression never changed. She looked neither amused nor aggravated. Hannah was sticking to the constipated theory.

"Beware," was the only answer she gave. It was low and growled, and the menacing tone brought shivers to Hannah's bare skin, despite the warmth of the water.

Another rustle drew her attention, and Hannah's eyes darted away, afraid she might also see Orlan Varela in her private sanctuary. She crossed her hands over her chest, just in case.

No one was there. And when she looked back, neither was Gouyen.

Somehow, however, her paperback had slipped into the tub, and the medicine bag had taken its place to balance on the rim.

"*That*, I understand!" Hannah whispered aloud. "Keep the bag with me, at all times."

CHAPTER 17

Hannah didn't make it to the second performance of the day, but she summoned the energy to attend the evening show. Walker offered to work the gate, and Fred stayed with Sadie at the inn, allowing Hannah to slip into the stands just as the first skit began. Shortly afterward, Walker joined her.

She hadn't arrived in time to speak with Jazz before the show. The few crewmembers she saw waved at her and made silly expressions, as if to say they were shocked to see her there, or to learn of her hidden riding skills, or both. Only two people made a point of speaking with her. Madge to express her concern, and Daphne to express her ire. That had been her favorite sequined top.

She caught glimpses of Shelton as he worked behind the scenes of the show, but his beloved Ladybird was conspicuously absent. Hannah was surprised to see that Tilly had returned to the lineup and that none of the acts were sacrificed.

"I have to hand it to you, Hannah," Walker said, leaning over during Ted McCavish's musical act. "This show is great. I was skeptical at first, but these are some top-notch performances. That man up there can really sing."

"Yes, he has an excellent voice," she agreed.

"Do they have the same skits each time?"

"No," she was pleased to say. "Some of this is different from last night. Which is good, because quite a few of these people are repeat customers."

"Which means they liked it well enough to come back. Good call by bringing them here."

"Thanks," she said, trying not to sound smug. "I've been very pleased so far. Well, all except for the incident with Shelton's horse."

"Shelton's horse? What happened with it?"

She stared at him in amazement. "Hello? Need I remind you? The whole runaway horse fiasco from this afternoon. You couldn't have forgotten it already!"

"Not at all. But that was a show horse, not Long's."

"No," she corrected. "That was his beloved Ladybird."

Walker looked confused. "He kept saying *his horse* this afternoon, but I thought he meant a horse under his care."

"No, he meant the horse that he loves like family. I actually saw them exchange kisses this afternoon." Now that she thought about it, the same lips that kissed the horse had also kissed hers. The thought was disturbing.

"*Why* were you riding Long's horse in the grand entry? Why weren't your riding one of the show's horses?"

"Actually, it kinda sorta is. Long story, but yesterday, we had to substitute Shelton's horse for Tilly. It was last minute, but it saved the day."

Hannah wasn't fooled by his calm demeanor. He appeared to be assimilating the facts, *before* he blew up. His voice was measured and low. "And who's Tilly?"

Even as Hannah nodded to the horse in the skit, the one Tim sang his lovelorn ballad to, a sick feeling formed in the pit of her stomach. "That—That one." She bit her lower lip. "She appears to have recovered."

On the bright side, Walker didn't scrub the back of his neck.

Instead, he squeezed the bridge of his nose and slowly shook his head. "Hannah." One word told her how bad it was. "Long's horse isn't on the insurance policy we bought for the show."

"No, but it's covered under my standard insurance, right?

"There was very specific language in the contract. It clearly specified that each and every animal has to be covered under the policy we purchased through *Hats Off*. It was overkill in my opinion, but they do a thorough well-animal checkup and have extremely high standards for their animals."

"I'm sure Shelton takes excellent care of his horse. It's not like it carries some sort of disease or something."

"It's not that," he argued. Around them, the crowd hooted with laughter, making it difficult to carry on a conversation. "We'll talk about this later," he said, his tone clipped.

"I'm sorry. I should have called you, but you were in that meeting, and I didn't want to disturb you. I thought I could handle this on my own."

"We've talked about this, Hannah. Never sign anything without reading the fine print."

"There were no papers! We verbally agreed to it. I never signed a thing."

"You signed the original contract, Hannah," he told her wearily. "The one that required buying their specific policies."

She gulped down the panic that rose in her throat. "Maybe nothing will come of it."

"Something will come on it," he all but growled.

"You don't know that."

They stared straight ahead, neither seeing the skit playing out on the stage. Pierce did a series of small magic tricks, wowing the crowd with his charisma and his skills.

"I do," Walker insisted.

"How?"

"Because I know Long. Believe me, he'll make something of it."

As Pierce called up volunteers from the audience—women this time, both sporting large handbags—Walker muttered under his breath. "I wouldn't be surprised if Long wasn't behind this whole thing."

"Oh, come on!" Hannah protested, hearing his complaint. "Don't be ridiculous. Shelton couldn't possibly have had anything to do with this mess."

"How do you know?"

"He wasn't even the one to suggest using his horse. Pierce was. Jazz brought up the insurance angle, so I suggested that Shelton 'sell' her his horse for the weekend, so that it was on her policy and satisfied terms of insurance. But he was adamantly against it. He was afraid she might try to claim legal ownership of the horse. Like he pointed out, he doesn't know her from Adam."

Walker pierced her with a scathing look. "So, your first inclination was to commit insurance fraud?"

She squirmed in her seat, as the crowd around them quietened. Talia had blindfolded the women on stage and engaged them in conversation, while Pierce made a show of sneaking their purses backstage. When he

returned with two very different purses, the crowd snickered in anticipation. No doubt, the bags were filled with
hilarious items that the blindfolded women would have to
identify.

"Not fraud, exactly," she denied, her voice a
hissed whisper. "Just a shortcut."

"But he refused to go along with it."

"That's right. Because the horse meant too much
to him. That's how I know he had nothing to do with today. There's no way he would risk the safety of his
beloved horse!"

Walker gave a grunt of agreement. "You're probably right about that."

The laughter picked up around them as the women
on stage reached into their handbags and brought out
items, one by one, that made no logical sense. Some of
their guesses had people practically rolling in the aisles
with fits of laughter.

"Tell me again, how did the horse make it into the
show?" Walker couldn't quite give up the troublesome
line of thought.

Her voice was small. "I talked him into it."

By the second half of the show, Hannah squirmed
uncomfortably in the stands. "Do you need to leave?"
Walker offered. "I can take you back to the inn."

"No. I want to see this chuck wagon skit again.
I'm still trying to figure out how they switch the people in
the wagons."

"Remember what Jazz told us? Trickery. Things
are not as they seem."

"I know, but I still like trying to figure it out."

"For starters, they probably used the twins. Have
one hide in the back of the wagon going in, the other hide

in a different wagon going out. They make the switch while the dust is swirling, or while you're watching something else. Trickery."

"Twins?"

"Ted and Tom. It's hard to tell them apart." He saw the surprised look on her face. "You didn't know?"

"No. I've never seen Tom. At least," she said with a sudden frown, "I don't think I have." She batted at his arm in frustration. "Besides, we can't leave before the final act. If you thought my ride was spectacular today, you should see Jazz and Pierce! They are amazing."

"Daphne tells me they're an item."

Hannah nodded. "Much to Daphne's disappointment. Daphne has the hots for Pierce," she explained.

"I think Daphne has the hots for any man in jeans," Walker grunted.

Hannah looked up at him and grinned. "She hit on you, didn't she, while you two were working the gate?"

Walker was clearly uncomfortable. "Maybe."

"You old charmer, you!" she teased. She bumped her arm against his, until she found that it hurt to do so. With evening setting in, she began to ache all over. She might have to take a second bath, and double up on the salts.

"I learned something else from her. She thinks that Rusty's death may not have been as accidental as the sheriff first thought."

"Really? Why?"

"Because Rusty had about as many enemies as he did friends. And he owed his roommate a lot of money. He kept saying he was working on a plan that would make them both rich. She seemed to think he was trying to blackmail someone on the crew."

"Who?"

"He never said. She thinks someone may have killed him to keep him silent."

Hannah frowned. Her fingers played with the small leather pouch in her pants pocket. Murder definitely qualified as evil.

"Then again, maybe she just has an over-active imagination," Walker said. "She also mentioned that the same roommate may have done something to get Rusty fired, so that his brother would get the job. She came short of accusing him of murder. She hinted that maybe he slipped something into his beer, and that Rusty had a bad reaction to it."

"I suppose anything is possible," Hannah agreed.

"She invited me back to her trailer tonight, to go over 'possible theories.'" His look of skepticism spoke volumes.

"Hey, don't worry about me," she offered with a laugh. "I can get back to the inn on my own."

"After the day you've had? As your friend and at- torney, I feel duty-bound to see you safely home."

Hannah grinned. "Think she'll fall for it?"

"That's the line I used, anyway."

"Do you think we should say something to the sheriff? If there was foul play, and the show moves on, they might never find the truth."

"You're right. They've already ruled it a natural death, and no one else would be the wiser."

"Maybe you should call the sheriff tomorrow. Oh, look, there's Jazz. Shh, we need to watch this."

The trick riding was as intriguing the second night as it had been the first. When the show was over, Walker grabbed Hannah's hand and led her down the crowded bleachers.

"Where are we going?"

"To check on Long's four-legged girlfriend. I want to see for myself if she's really hurt."

"Holy boomtown, you don't still suspect him of doing something underhanded, do you?" She was clearly exasperated.

"I absolutely do. I wouldn't put a thing past Long."

"What is it with you two?" she demanded. She stopped in the middle of the walkway, refusing to budge until he stopped and turned her way. "Why do you distrust him so?"

"Because he's a weasel."

"Then why did you hire him to shoe the horses?"

"Because weasel or not, he's good with animals," Walker admitted. "His talents just don't extend to people."

"You're impossible!" she muttered, but as someone bumped into her from behind, she allowed him to tug her forward.

Ignoring the barriers intended to keep non-personnel away, they wiggled their way through narrow openings and orange netting. They reached the livestock pen at the back of the arena, where the horses enjoyed an after-work treat of specialized grains.

Three pens down, they found Ladybird. Colorful, custom-made bindings wrapped her legs. A matching fleece cooler covered her back as she lay on a clean bed of hay.

"Only the best for his girl, I see," Walker murmured in sarcasm.

A sharp "Hey!" drew their attention. Shelton Long scurried their way, his long legs eating up the distance. "Get away from my horse!" He broke into a lope as Walker stood stubbornly in place.

Hannah felt the need to speak. "I'm sorry about today, Shelton. I don't know what happened. When we started for the exit, she broke into a gallop. I was so busy trying not to fall off, I may have jerked her. And then—then she just went berserk and tried to buck me off!"

"Her leg got tangled in the guy-line," he said, defending his horse. "She was trying to get free, not buck you off." His eyes went to the horse's hind leg. "She has a pretty deep gash, where the wire cut into her leg."

"I noticed she wasn't in the show tonight."

"Dr. Hogan advised against it."

Beside her, Hannah felt Walker stiffen. She made a mental note to ask him about it later.

For the first time since the incident, Shelton turned to her in concern. "Are you all right? I know I didn't show it earlier, but I really am concerned about you." He caught her wrist and stepped closer, turning his body to exclude Walker from the conversation. His voice dropped a note. "When I saw my horse lying there, obviously in so much pain, I admit I panicked. I didn't express my full concern on your behalf. I apologize for that."

Hannah ignored Walker's snort. She didn't recall the horse being in any significant pain earlier, but in truth, she had been more concerned with her own safety than with the horse's.

"I understand," she said kindly. "You're very attached to your horse, and you were worried. And as it turned out, I was fine. Walker saw to that." She worked her wrist out of Shelton's hold. "He pulled me from the horse, before I fell off. Walker may have very well saved my life."

Instead of looking grateful, the man glared at her companion. "That explains the bruise to Ladybird's flank. When you jerked the saddle, the girth bit into her and left a mark."

Walker brushed the other man aside and all but grabbed Hannah's arm. He thrust it forward to reveal the burgeoning bruise on her forearm. "Hannah received multiple bruises." His voice was cold. "That happened when your horse broke rank, got herself tangled in a mess of her own making, and raced across the open pasture at will. The outcome could have been much worse. For that horse," he jabbed a finger toward Ladybird, "and for Hannah."

"Don't try to blame this on my horse!"

"The blame is entirely on your horse!"

The two men stood toe to toe, their faces within inches of one another. For one terrible moment, Hannah thought it might come to blows.

"This is about Doc, ain't it?" Shelton jeered. "You can't stand it, because she sided with me!"

"You influenced her testimony, and you know it."

"She gave her opinion, exactly like the judge ordered her to do."

"She changed her opinion when you two started dating."

"You just couldn't stand it, could you? The fact that she chose me, over you!"

Behind them, Hannah gasped. They both turned to her in surprise, having forgotten she was present.

"A woman!" she spat. "That's what's behind this ridiculous vendetta you two have? A woman?" Her fingers curled into fists, and fire flashed from her blue eyes. She started to stomp away but whirled around to give them a parting word of advice. "Grow up! Both of you!"

***

"Hannah! Hannah, wait!"

She heard Walker calling her name as she hurried from the livestock area. She was too angry to face him right now. Angry, and sore, and hurt. She wasn't certain which of the three took precedence.

Earlier today, her heart had warmed at the way Walker took up for *her*. Not as a possession, not as a pawn, but as a person.

But now the truth came out. The real reason he objected to Shelton. Not because of the farrier's lack of character, or because of an old lawsuit, or even because of her. He wasn't jealous over *her* and Shelton. He was jealous over *another woman* and Shelton!

What is it with men? Why are they so childish? Always posturing. Always so competitive, fighting to be the fastest, the strongest, the best. They couldn't stand to be outdone, particularly in the romance department.

Was that the real reason Shelton Long seemed determined to pursue her? Sure, they had talked several times over the phone this week, but he seemed to think they had established some sort of relationship. One kiss did not a romance make. While she hadn't completely shut down his advances, she hadn't particularly encouraged them, either. Did he keep asking her out because he genuinely liked her, or because he knew it would get under Walker's skin? Was she just another rung on his ladder of competition with the lawyer?

And who, Hannah had to wonder, was this woman, the one that had caused such open hostility between the men? Walker must have truly cared for her, a fact that pricked at Hannah's heart.

Worst of all was this sting of disappointment she felt; it forced her to acknowledge a side of Walker she didn't think existed. After getting to know the attorney and the kind of man she *thought* he was, Hannah found herself disillusioned. Of all people, she thought Walker was above such pettiness. She expected more of him.

Just goes to show, she thought, clicking her tongue.

People can fool you, every time.

CHAPTER 18

Sunday Brunch brought another full house to the *Spirits of Texas Inn*. Hannah went through the motions of personally greeting and visiting with the guests, but her mind was elsewhere.

Last night, Hannah had taken her second soaking bath of the day. She had added extra bath salts and extra wine, hoping to heal her wounded pride, alongside her wounded body. When daylight burst into her room a few scant hours later, she had a slight hangover, one slightly bruised ego, and a host of new aches and pains.

As she spoke to guests and refilled water glasses, Hannah ran through the list that played like ticker tape in her head. *Check guests out by noon... clean rooms... more towels for the Elliotts... check supplies for the coming week... confirm new bookings... tally up with Jazz after the matinee and write final check... book them again for next year... ask Walker if he remembered to call the sheriff's office... smile at the women coming this way...*

"Hello!" the younger of the women said, her smile warm and friendly. She thrust her hand forward for a proper greeting. "We've not met, not officially, but we've talked over the phone. I'm Tracey Ann Crenwelge. This is my mother, Maureen."

"Tracey…? Oh, from the sheriff's office. You're the dispatcher." *The one not so secretly infatuated with Walker and the one who probably thinks I'm a kook. How was I supposed to know the intruder I reported was actually a ghost?* Anyone could have made the mistake.

"You sure know how to stir things up, don't you?" Tracey Ann grinned. Taking a seat at the newly cleared table, she explained to her companion, "This is Hannah, the new owner. She's only been here a few months, and already she's called in an intruder, a break-in, two armed assailants, and now a death. Usually my job is rather boring—mostly reports of fender benders and people hitting deer—but this one here keeps things hopping!"

"It's not as if I'm actually responsible for any of those things happening," Hannah pointed out in self-defense. "I just make the phone call."

"It's the most excitement we've seen on this side of the county in ages! And now you've brought all those carnies into town." She wiggled in excitement. "I'm having so much fun, running their backgrounds!"

"Uhm… er… what do you mean?"

"Oh, some of those *Hats Off* crew are real characters, if you know what I mean." Tracey Ann cupped her mouth, her whisper too loud to be construed as confidential. "Most have criminal records."

Hannah swallowed hard. She had planned to invite the troupe back next year, but if what Tracey Ann said was true… She pulled out a chair and slid into it without invitation. "That doesn't sound good. Maybe you should tell me more."

"Well," Tracey Ann said with a dramatic flair, clearly loving the attention. She leaned forward to give her words more weight. "I can't name names, of course, but one of the men served six years in the pen for insurance fraud. Two brothers have records of domestic abuse and battery. Almost all of them are wanted for tax evasion or child support, or at least some sort of petty crime. And one of the women has more ex-husbands than I have freckles!"

Hannah listened worriedly. It would have been nice to have this information before now. *Before* she booked their services and brought them to town! "And the owner? What do you know about her?"

Tracey Ann tossed her blond head and happily supplied the information. Hannah wondered how much was public knowledge, and how much 'privileged' information. Tracey Ann might need to brush up on the department's privacy and non-disclosure policies.

But not before she gave Hannah the scoop on Jazz.

"Diane Jasmine Dawson, thirty-two, originally from Phoenix, and more or less born into show business. Her mother was an acrobat in Vegas, her dad a rodeo bum. When they were kids, Jazz—as she's now known—and her younger brother had a little act they performed on the street. They were apparently good enough to go out on the road and played all over the Southwest. The act fell apart when Jazz was offered a spot in Vegas. Trick riding in one of those shows with the flashy horses."

"What happened to the brother?"

"I couldn't find much on the brother. Their parents split up soon after. Jazz stayed with their father, and David, the brother, went with the mother."

"So, Jazz's record is clean?" Hannah asked.

So far, it sounded as if Jazz might be one of those good-hearted people who hired less fortunate, down-on-their-luck lost souls and offered them a second chance.

"I didn't find anything of significance on her. But get this. Dad was a small-time scam artist. While the kids dazzled the audience with music and magic tricks, Dad helped himself to their pockets. He left a string of arrests in every town they toured."

"Great role model," Hannah murmured. She looked at Tracey Ann and asked, "How did you say you know all this? More importantly, *why* do you know all this?"

"A formality, really," the dispatcher assured her. "Background checks on the cast and crew. The sheriff is ninety-five percent certain that poor man died of natural causes. But," she added, with a wiggle of her eyebrows, "there's always that five percent!"

Hannah nibbled on her lip. "Now that you mention it, there's something the sheriff may need to know about the case. Walker plans to call him today."

"Oh, sheriff's out fishing today."

"Can I report it to you, then?"

"To me?" Tracy Ann's initial look of surprise gave way to flattery. "Why, yes. Yes, of course. I'm not on duty, but of course, you can give me the information. I'll make certain the sheriff gets it, first thing in the morning."

"It can't wait that long. The show is set to pull out this afternoon, so by then, it would be too late."

"Too late for what?"

Hannah wondered if she were doing the right thing. Was she stirring up trouble where there was none? Was Daphne a reliable source, or an over-zealous gossip? In the end, Hannah went with her gut feeling. There could be no harm in sharing what little she knew. It would be up to the sheriff whether to pursue it.

"The thing is… one of the cast members thinks there may be something more to Rusty's death than meets the eye."

"Are you saying she believes there's *more* than a five percent chance this man didn't really have a heart attack?"

Hannah nodded. "From what I understand, that's exactly what she believes."

Tracy Ann clapped her hands together in delight, her eyes twinkling. "You see, Mom?" she said, turning to the older woman. "I told you Hannah keeps things hopping! Now she's brought us a murder!"

Hannah started to deny the ridiculous claim, but something held her back. Technically, she *was* responsible for bringing the show to town, so in a manner of speaking, she *had* brought a murderer into their midst.

If, indeed, the poor man had been murdered, she reminded herself. They didn't know for certain yet. Before excusing herself, Hannah thanked Tracey Ann for the information and for relaying her message to the sheriff.

As she wove her way through the tables, nodding and smiling at other guests as her mind raced miles ahead, a woman snagged her arm.

"I'm Barbara Schuleter," the woman said with a broad smile. "I just want to tell you what a fine job you've done here, revitalizing the old inn."

"Why, thank you. I take it you live in the area?"

"A few miles south of here, closer to Sisterdale. My husband and I were so excited when we learned you were bringing back the weekend brunches! That Sadie Tanner is one fine cook."

"Yes, she certainly is."

She dipped her fork into a pile of thin, crispy potato pancakes and brought it up for dreamy examination. "It's been much too long since I've had her *kartoffelpuff-er*. They're just like Mama used to make."

Hannah noticed a vacated spot with a half-filled juice glass beside the other woman. "Is your husband with you today?"

It took her a moment to answer, but Barbara nodded emphatically while she chewed. She had been unable to resist the temptation, popping the crepe-like pancake into her mouth. Swallowing, she said, "He was even more excited about the brunch than I was! He's getting his second plate now."

Her comment gave Hannah pause. Did they have a limit on refills, or was the buffet all you can eat? As owner, that was definitely something she should know. She'd put that on the ticker tape, too… *ask Sadie if we're losing money on the buffet… consider buying smaller plates…*

"Tell me something, dear," Barbara said, putting the fork down and propping her elbows unapologetically upon the table. "I'll be quick, before Harvey gets back. He doesn't believe in such, but I hear the inn has some, shall we say, *special guests*."

"Actually, we consider all of our guests special," Hannah sincerely answered.

"Oh, of course, but I mean… okay, I'll just say it. The inn is rumored to have ghosts." She all but quivered in excitement. "Is that true?"

Unsure of how to answer, Hannah did the next best thing. She hedged. "Actually, I've heard those same rumors myself."

"And?" The eager expression on Barbara Schuleter's face turned suddenly to disappointment. "Oh, here comes Harvey, and he doesn't like me talking about such things." Her voice dropped to a conspiratorial whisper. "Just give me a quick yes or no."

Hannah turned and watched as an older gentleman approached the table. It wasn't the over-flowing plate that snagged Hannah's attention. (Although getting smaller buffet plates suddenly moved up a few slots on her mental ticker tape list.) It was the woman on his arm that she first noticed.

Decked out in her Southern belle finery, Caroline floated gracefully by his side, like royalty being escorted into the room. Her dainty hand snugged into the crook of his arm, and she wore a smile upon her face. She looked every bit the queen of the ball, except for two minor facts. One, her feet glided several inches off the floor. And two, Harvey Schuleter had no inkling of the spirit's presence.

Biting back a giggle, Hannah addressed Harvey's wife. "Let's just say, I'll keep my eyes open."

The man set his plate on the table and hefted his considerable bulk into the chair, but not before a shiver ran through his shoulders. "Are you okay sitting here?" he asked his wife. "Seems a mite drafty, if you ask me."

Barbara waved her hand in dismissal. "I'm quite comfortable. I was just chatting with the new owner, Hannah… what was your last name, dear? This is my husband, Harvey."

"Duncan. Hannah Duncan. It's a pleasure to meet you, Mr. Schuleter."

They exchanged pleasantries and small talk before Hannah bid them good day. As she moved on with the rest of her duties, a flash of yellow caught her eye. Caroline sat at the table with the Sanchez family now, exchanging silly faces with the little boy.

***

With another successful brunch over, all departing guests checked out, and things at the inn quiet, Hannah had a few moments to spare before working the gate at the final matinee performance of *Hats Off*.

Despite what Tracey Ann had told her about much of the cast and crew, she still felt that bringing the show to the town of Hannah had been a good call. All five shows had seen a sell-out crowd, meaning more exposure for the inn. With the public obviously enjoying every moment, it created a good camaraderie with her neighbors and made the favorable first impression she had hoped for. She had definitely *Gone Big.*

She had to admit, Shelton Long had played a big part in this weekend's success. If he hadn't pitched in to take the wrangler's place, and if he hadn't offered his prize horse as a last-minute replacement, things may have gone quite differently. Hannah was still skeptical of whether his interest in her was sincere—and uncertain of how she felt about it, if it were—but nonetheless felt she owed the man a sincere and proper thank you. Immediately after the show, she determined she would find him and tell him so.

"That was quite a ride you had yesterday," Daphne said. Considering she was Hannah's partner at the gate today, it was a good thing she had dropped her grudge over the ruined shirt.

"I'm still feeling the effects of it," Hannah admitted. With a rueful smile, she indicated the cushioned pad beneath her.

"It could have turned out worse," the redhead pointed out.

"Very true."

"So, tell me something. Which one of those hunky men are you with? The hot lawyer, or the handsome horse whisperer?"

Hannah's reply was quick and terse. "Neither."

"I've never seen anything quite like what happened yesterday. The way that lawyer came racing to your rescue…" She used hand gestures and dramatic enunciation to make her point. "He came racing through the scene, scattered trail riders every which way, jumped a barrier, and shot out into the pasture. It was just like in the movies! And then the way Shelton took off running on foot, until Jazz came along and gave him a ride." She laughed, a dreamy expression on her face. "I tell ya, I wish I had two men that looked like them chasing after me, instead of… ” She seemed to think better of finishing her thought, ending with, “…well, I just wish I had those two. Or even one or the other.” With a coarse laugh, she added, “Despite rumors to the contrary, I ain't greedy.”

“But you *do* have men chasing after you,” Hannah pointed out. She suspected Daphne was the one with the string of ex-husbands Tracey Ann had mentioned.

Now that she thought about it, this was the perfect opportunity to ask the performer some questions. She could find out how reliable of a source the woman was, or if she had passed her suspicions along for nothing. If Daphne turned out to be nothing but a gossip, or had made up the claims for Walker's benefit, she could always call Tracey Ann and tell her to forget about the tip.

“I hear Guy leads the chase,” Hannah said. “I understand he's one of your most avid admirers.”

Daphne shrugged. “Where'd you hear that?”

“Several people mentioned it, actually. That must have been a little awkward for you, since he and Rusty were best friends and all. I understand you and Rusty weren't very close?” She made it a question.

“You could say that.”

“Any particular reason?”

Daphne all but hooted. “Did you ever meet the man? All he ever did was complain. No matter what it was, it didn't suit him. Not many people did get along with him, if you want to know the truth.”

“What about Guy? I understand they were best friends and roommates, but still had a tumultuous relationship.”

“If that means they fought a lot, then, yeah. They had a tumbled relationship.”

Hannah bit back a smile, not bothering to correct her. She lowered her voice to ask, “Just between us, do you think Guy could have had anything to do with his death?"

Daphne denied it, but Hannah could hear the note of doubt in her voice. "Guy's a hothead, but surely he wouldn't… I mean, he's harmless. Mostly. I don't think he'd really do it, even if he did threaten to a time or two."

The revelation surprised Hannah. "He actually threatened to kill his roommate?" She couldn't keep the shock from her voice.

"Maybe," she admitted, not quite meeting Hannah's eyes. A group of people came through the line, interrupting further comment. By the time they moved on, Daphne must have felt the need to defend her suitor.

"It's just that Guy was awfully upset," she explained, "when he found out Rusty had blackmailed me a couple of times."

The surprises just kept coming. "Rusty blackmailed you? Whatever for?"

"Well," the performer admitted with a coy smile, "I may have led one or two fellas on. At the same time. But a woman gets lonely, you know, living on the road all the time. Rusty may have found out a time or two, and tried to make a few dollars off my loneliness."

"Was he blackmailing you when he died?"

"No, ma'am, not me. I learned my lesson the last time. Even if Rusty wasn't bleeding me dry, it was too nerve wracking, seeing two brothers at one time. But somehow, Guy found out—not about his brother, thank God, but about the blackmail scheme—and he was furious with Rusty."

Holy boomtown! This is no more than a traveling soap opera!

Hannah schooled the shock from showing on her face. Daphne was not only John Boy's ex and Guy's wanna-be, but she dallied with Guy's brother behind his back. And all the while, she tried to hook up with Pierce.

*Geesh. When does she find time to practice her routine?
Or sleep?*

"I don't think he would carry through with his
threat," Daphne continued, "but… I just don't know. With
his hot temper, sometimes Guy scares me."

"You should talk to the police and tell them your
concerns."

Guy, of all people, chose that moment to walk up.
Hannah didn't think he had overheard their conversation,
but she couldn't be certain. She watched for a telltale sign
on his face that he might be upset, but he only seemed
concerned with Daphne.

"Hey, there, gorgeous," he said. He thrust a cold
drink forward. "I thought you might enjoy a little something cold. It's already getting mighty warm."

"Why, thank you, sugar. What a sweet thing to
do!" Daphne purred the words as she curled her long body
into a seductive pose. "I was just telling Hannah here
what a sweetheart you were. Isn't that right, Hannah?
Weren't we just talking about this handsome hunk of a
man?"

"Uhm, yes. Yes, that's exactly right."

Clearly flattered, he wanted to hear more. "Yeah?
What were you saying about me?"

Before Daphne could babble more coquettish nonsense, Hannah piped in. "We were saying how hard it
must be for you, losing your best friend and roommate."

His demeanor immediately changed. "What were
you talking about that for?" he asked gruffly. "What was
between Rusty and me is none of your business!"

Seeing the flash of anger in his eyes—he *was* a
hothead!—Hannah quickly fabricated a response. "Daphne was worried you might become depressed."

"I'm depressed that my brother didn't get the head
wrangler job," he grumbled. His glower deepened. "After
all we did for her, and then she goes and gives the job to

an outsider! It just ain't right!" He kicked at a loose clump of grass. "We're good enough to do all her dirty work for her, but not good enough to get promotions. I've been working for the same measly pay for the past three years."

Daphne shot a *now look what you've done* frown to Hannah. To Guy, she purred, "Aw, don't be like that, sugar. Shelton Long isn't staying on. This was just a one-thing time. And I have a feeling that after the show in Palestine next weekend, we'll all be getting a raise. I overheard the top brass talking. Something about after next week, money wouldn't be a problem anymore."

"Don't mean they'll share a dime with us," Guy grumbled, but his expression lightened somewhat.

"They said there'd be enough to go around. I figure that means we'll all get a raise."

Hannah turned to greet a family of five as they came through the line. As showtime drew closer and the crowd picked up, there was no more time for conversation.

CHAPTER 19

The cast bowed for their second standing ovation as Hannah made her way out of the stands. As this was the final performance, there was no carnival this afternoon. Instead, the fans were invited to come down and mingle with the cast for last-minute selfies and scribbled autographs. Hannah navigated the crowd, intent on checking on Ladybird. She had seen Jeff herding the horses toward the back, which meant the farrier should be there, too.

Jeff. Guy's brother. The heir-apparent to the head wrangler throne. Hannah cataloged the thoughts in her head as she walked. Was Jeff one of the brothers with the domestic abuse rap sheet?

A feeling of unease moved through her shoulders.

More importantly, could *Jeff* have been the one to kill Rusty? Not only did he covet the late wrangler's position, but he also had reason to keep him silent. He wouldn't want his brother to know of his affair with Daphne.

As the saying goes, Hannah thought, *dead men tell no tales*.

When she rounded the corner and spotted Shelton unsaddling the horses without help, she breathed a little easier. At least for now, Jeff was nowhere to be seen.

The lanky farrier whistled a tune as he worked. Hannah vaguely recognized it as a show tune, although his rendition had a slightly different beat, and added bars. Come to think of it, she decided, maybe it wasn't a tune she recognized. That, or he was terrible at whistling.

"Shelton?"

He looked up when she called his name. A slow, pleased smile spread across his face. Could he fake such pleasure at seeing her, she wondered. Or did it please him because she sought him out? He might see it as being one step ahead of the lawyer in the race for the innkeeper's heart.

Get over yourself, girlfriend. It's not your heart they're fighting over.

"Hey, Hannah. I'm glad you came. I was going to look you up, just as soon as I finished up here."

"How's Ladybird today?"

The smile fell from his face. "I'm worried about her. The vet is on her way now. I can't see any obvious damage, but she's still limping. I'm worried it may be nerve damage."

"That doesn't sound good."

Neither did having the doctor on the premises. For whatever reason, Hannah didn't look forward to meeting the other woman, especially knowing she had once been someone important in Walker's life.

She pictured the vet in her mind's eye. Small, petite, with flawless skin, and long flaxen hair. A figure to die for. A scintillating combination of femininity and intelligence, making her virtually impossible to compete with.

Hannah shook her head, knocking the foolish thought from her head. There was no competition.

Shelton was still talking about his horse, spouting off possible scenarios and their horrific consequences.

"Shelton. Just calm down. Breathe." A smile played with the corners of her mouth. "Isn't that what you told me, when I got hysterical?"

Finished with taking the rigging from the last horse, he slapped it on the rump to send it on its way. The horse went straight to the feed trough, where its companions were currently huddled. Shelton brushed his hands clean as he sauntered her way.

His smile was fifty percent amusement, fifty percent confidence. One hundred percent charm.

"Feel free to use my foolproof method of stopping hysterical rants," he offered, stopping just in front of her. Only the corral railing separated them.

Hannah stood on tiptoe to brush a kiss against his cheek.

"Slightly less effective than my preferred method," he said with a pretend scowl, "but acceptable."

"I came by to thank you, Shelton."

He looked genuinely surprised. "For what?"

"For saving this weekend. Without you, it could have been a complete disaster."

"Nah, I didn't do all that much."

"Are you kidding? You rearranged your schedule, forfeited your entire weekend, and went above and beyond the call of duty. You took on a difficult task and made it look easy. You donated your time and effort, your expertise with animals, and then, to top it off, you donated your prized horse. My biggest regret is that Ladybird got hurt in the process."

"And yet, all you offer me as thanks is a peck on the cheek?" he teased. "Surely, you can do better than that." His long arms slipped around her waist and drew her against the fence.

Before Hannah could contemplate the next step, they heard someone approaching.

"I'm sorry I'm late getting here. How's our patient today?"

The blond man dropped his arms from around her and vaulted over the fence, making the feat look effortless. "Hey, Doc. Thanks for coming." His attention shifted to the other woman, but his concern was for his horse. "I'm worried. She's worse today. Laid out on her side, like something hurts."

"Is she eating?"

"She hasn't touched the bucket of grains, and they're her favorite blend." As an afterthought, he remembered Hannah's presence. "Have you met my friend? Hannah, this is Gabriella. The best veterinarian in Gillespie County. Gaby, meet Hannah Duncan."

A friendly smile spread across the veterinarian's face, and she extended her hand for a hearty handshake. Hannah reminded herself to close her gaping mouth.

Gabriella Hogan was nothing as she had imagined. With her hair stuffed entirely beneath a battered cap, it was difficult to know whether it was long or short. The few tendrils that escaped were hardly flaxen. Bright red was a more accurate description. Freckles graced the bridge of her nose and scattered along her arms and hands. Gabriella was every bit as tall as Hannah was, and had a full figure. Her hips were wider than were considered vogue, but Hannah had to admit, the woman definitely knew how to fill out a pair of jeans.

"Pleasure to meet you, Hannah. I love what you're doing here with Miss Wilhelmina's legacy, keeping the inn going and all. And smart move, getting Shelton to step in for the show. If anyone knows horses, it's this man."

She barely gave Hannah time to reply before she turned to Shelton, her manner becoming more professional. "Let's go check on our patient. I don't mind telling you, I'm worried about her. Visibly, there's no apparent damage. Which leads me to suspect it could be something internal, or, worse, nerve damage."

Shelton was visibly distraught. "That sounds serious."

The veterinary didn't mince words. "It could be debilitating. I won't know until I run a full battery of tests."

"Spare no expense, Doc," he said. His voice turned hard. "I'll sell everything I have to get her the best care. And then I'll sue *Hats Off*, until they have to sell everything they have, too."

"Walk with me. Hannah, it was a pleasure. I'm sure I'll be seeing you around."

"I'll be back," Shelton promised, squeezing Hannah's arm.

It was difficult to peg their relationship just by watching them. Gabriella didn't appear to be jealous, nor had Shelton seemed guilty about being seen hugging another woman. There was no flirting on either of their part. In truth, it appeared they were little more than friends. If they had ever had a romantic relationship, it seemed to have fizzled out now.

Not that she spent much time contemplating the disappearing couple. She had bigger things to worry about. Namely, what if Shelton decided to sue her, too? She had agreed to cover the horse on her insurance policy, and the incident happened on Hannah property.

More worried now than ever, Hannah turned and came face to face with Jazz. John Boy was only steps behind.

"Hannah. Just the person I wanted to see."

Something about Jazz's voice and cool smile—the steel in them, perhaps?—put Hannah on edge. Nonetheless, she offered a cordial smile in return. "Great show, as always."

"Thank you. I trust you've recovered from yesterday's ordeal?" Jazz's eyes swept over her, looking for signs of injury.

"More or less," Hannah said. With a rueful smile, she rubbed her backside.

"We need to talk." Her tone was abrupt.

Wariness moved into Hannah's voice. "I'm listening."

"As this was our last show, we'll need to settle your account before we move out."

Hannah was slow to nod. "Yes, that was my understanding."

"Normally, we would tally the proceeds from the gate, apply potential credit from trailer sales, and deduct the appropriate amount from your bill." The small blond woman held her back as stiffly as she held her voice. Her eyes settled upon Hannah's. "In this case, however, I'm afraid there will be no applied funds. This is my official demand for payment in full, due immediately."

Hannah's gasp was audible. "You can't be serious!"

"Believe me, Hannah, I always take money very seriously."

"But— You can't do that! We have a contract!"

Her reply was cold. "A contract which you broke."

"What—What are you talking about?"

Stay calm. Don't hyperventilate. Not now.

All traces of the warm country-girl persona had vanished. No trace of the sparkling, charismatic performer remained. Before her stood a shrewd, formal businesswoman. Her words were clipped and measured.

"You rode an unauthorized horse in the Grand Entry yesterday. After the damage it inflicted, I simply cannot allow this farce to continue. Our contract clearly states—"

"What damage?" Hannah interrupted.

"The horse managed to entangle itself in some of our wires. It pulled a guy-line loose, creating a possible hazard to the cast and crew. It also damaged a very valuable component to our sound system." When Hannah would have protested further, Jazz held up a hand to quiet her. "In addition, Mr. Long informs me that his horse sustained a deep laceration and possible permanent nerve damage to its leg. He insists that *Hats Off* cover all veterinary bills. Naturally, that cost will be passed on to you, as you agreed to be financially responsible for the animal."

"I'm sure my insurance will cover all associated costs," Hannah assured her.

"I demand no less." She managed to look down her nose at Hannah, even though the sprite of a woman was several inches shorter. "That, however, is a separate issue. The issue at hand is that you broke the contract. You did not provide the required insurance for the dapple mare."

Hannah was flabbergasted. Her incredulous expression said as much. "She was covered under my policy, just as we discussed!"

"The contract clearly states that all animals must be fully vetted and covered under the *Hats Off* policy you agreed to purchase. Any deviation can, and will, result in immediate remuneration for our services, in full, by the end of the business day. Voiding the contract relieves our organization of all legal, contractual, and financial responsibilities." She spouted off the words as easily as if she read them from a script.

Hannah tossed her hands in the air. "But you agreed to use the horse!"

"It may have escaped your notice, but Ladybird did not perform in Friday night's performance. Her introduction to the show came while *you* were riding her. A horse you failed to specifically list on the insurance policy, which clearly voids our contract."

Hannah narrowed her eyes as Tracey Ann's words again floated through her head.

…But get this. Dad was a small-time scam artist…

Had Jazz followed in her father's footsteps? Had she been duped? What if this had been some sort of elaborate scam, orchestrated to play out this way? For all she knew, Jazz made a habit of finding creative ways to break the contract. Declaring the contract null and void meant they could collect all proceeds from the gate and significantly increase their bottom line.

But surely, someone would have complained about such. Hannah read the reviews before booking the show, and no one mentioned any devious practices. Almost all had given them glowing reviews and a five-star rating

All which could have been fake, she realized.

"Look, Missy," John Boy interjected, breaking into her thoughts. He hiked his belt loops, looking for a moment like an Old West gunslinger, reaching for his six-shooter. "We don't want no trouble. We have a legally binding contract, and the law is on our side. Just ask your lawyer."

Eyes flashing, Hannah stepped forward and jabbed her finger into the man's chest. It was every bit as thick as his head. "I'm not your *Missy*, John *Boy*!" she spat. "And you can bet I'll ask my lawyer. I don't know what kind of scam you two have going, but you won't get away with it."

While John Boy made blustery noises of protest, Jazz smoothly replied, "We run a business, not a scam."

"We'll see about that!"

The blonde narrowed her eyes. "Are you threatening me?"

"No. I'm promising you a fight."

Jazz Dawson bared her teeth when she smiled. "Bring it on. *Missy*."

CHAPTER 20

Hannah was in no mood to entertain guests when she returned to the inn. She was in even less of a mood to see Orlan there, engaged in an imaginary shoot-out with young Eli Sanchez. The family was having such a good time, they had extended their reservation for one more day. The parents currently relaxed in the lounge with their e-readers, while Eli entertained himself.

She went straight to her office and plopped heavily into her desk chair. A quick call to Walker, explaining the essence of the problem, had the attorney on his way over.

When the door opened behind her several minutes later, she didn't bother opening her eyes. She could feel his anger. Smell his scent. Hear the gears churning in his brain, as he sought a solution to the mess she had created.

"What are we going to do?" she wailed.

His answer was honest. "I don't know."

Hannah turned the chair to face him, her face expressing how miserable she was.

"No offense, but you look terrible."

"Then I'm a matched set, because I'm in a terrible mood, too," she informed him.

"Can't say I don't feel the same way."

It was on her tongue to say he looked terrible, as well, but it simply wasn't true. As always, Walker was so devastatingly sexy, it made her hurt just a little bit, in that spot between her heart and her stomach. It created a painful hitch in her lungs, in that moment when she always forgot to breathe. And it hurt in her heart, because she knew his vendetta against Shelton Long involved another woman. A woman he obviously still cared about. A woman she had met and immediately liked, in spite of the situation.

So, instead of spouting empty lies, Hannah redirected her attention to more urgent matters than her pathetic love life.

"It's a scam, Walker," she said, her eyes now flashing with ire. "It has to be. I don't know how, but she orchestrated this entire thing. From the very beginning, she had no intention of paying me my share of the proceeds. I can't prove it, but I *know* it."

"But without proof…"

"Why else would there be such specific language in the contract? You said it was overkill. Unnecessary stipulations. Why would they be in the contract, unless they intended to use them against us?"

"I admit, it went above and beyond the norm, but it was hardly illegal. I made certain of that fact, before we signed a single paper."

She kept replaying the conversations in her head, trying to find a clue. Something that pointed to the organization being less than trustworthy. Something that hinted at a scam. The only conclusion she came to was that Jazz and crew were professional actors, and that she was too trusting.

"Somehow, they set me up," she insisted.

"Maybe," he agreed, but the word lacked confidence. "The good news is that as far as the vet bill for Ladybird goes, the horse is covered under your policy. At least there's no issue there."

"Because you personally know the vet?" She couldn't resist the jab.

He found no humor in her saccharine smile. "No, because you have adequate coverage."

Hannah stood and paced the room. "So, the trick was to get us to use a different horse, one not covered under their policy. It provided the perfect opportunity for them to renege on their end of the contract."

"Tell me again how the switch came about."

Hannah went through the details of the previous day, as she remembered them.

"Did you actually see Tilly limping?"

"Now that you mention it, no, I didn't." Her forehead puckered in a frown. "And she seemed to be fine today, didn't she?"

"Which may or may not mean a thing. On either account," he pointed out.

"No, but it makes sense. Fake an injury, pretend it has major consequences on the show, and act distraught." Hannah narrowed her eyes as she thought it through. "They're all trained actors. How hard would it be to fake a catastrophe? It gives them the perfect opportunity to bring in an unauthorized horse. Jazz even threw in the argument about insurance coverage to make it look more convincing, and probably to distract me. I was so busy thinking about the insurance angle, I forgot to worry about the contractual angle! But it was all rigged, right from the beginning!"

"So Long must be in on it, too."

"As much as you'd love to pin this on him, I think he's an innocent pawn in their game, same as me. You didn't see his face yesterday. He was clearly against using his horse, mainly because he didn't trust Jazz." Her lips took a downturn. "Turns out, he was right."

"Maybe," Walker grunted, still unconvinced. "If he was part of it, he got what he deserved. He may have sacrificed his beloved horse in the process."

"So what do we do now?"

"The way I see it, you have two choices. One, we can refuse to pay. They'll sue, of course, which could result in a long, expensive, drawn-out court battle."

"And the other choice?"

Walker reverted to scrubbing the back of his neck. Hannah hated the idea, before she even heard it. "You could pay the bill and be done with it. It would make a dent in the budget, but it wouldn't completely wreck it."

"But then I'd be admitting defeat, on my very first effort." Her voice was miserable. "And Jazz would get by with whatever scam it is she's running."

Walker hefted out a sigh. "So, what are you saying?"

A lift of her shoulder said there was only one clear answer. After all, she had chosen to *Go Big*. There was no way she would tuck her tail between her legs and go home.

Touching the leather amulet in her pocket, she felt a steely resolve stiffen her spine. She looked Walker straight in the eye and gave him a word one answer.

"Fight."

CHAPTER 21

Once again, he barged into her RV without knocking.

"When you said you'd take care of Rusty, what *exactly* did you mean?"

"Please, barge right in," she said dryly. "Don't mind me. It's just my trailer."

"Don't be cute with me. What did you mean about Rusty?"

"What do you think I meant? I meant I'd talk to him. Stress the importance of keeping his mouth shut."

"That's all?"

"Of course."

"And did you?"

"Talk to him? I didn't get a chance. Two hours later, he was dead."

"How did he die?"

"How should I know?" she snapped. "I'm no medical doctor. My guess is he had a heart attack. Assuming, of course, he had a heart."

"Where were you just now? I tried calling you. Knocked on your door."

"As you can see, I just got out of the shower."

"The sheriff deputy just left. They got a tip. Something about Rusty not dying of natural causes."

"You mean he may have been *murdered*?"

"That's the most unnatural way I can think of to die."

"Do they know what happened? Do they have a suspect?"

"Yeah. All of *us*. They left orders not to leave town for the foreseeable future."

"But we have a show next weekend in Palestine!"

"Not anymore, we don't."

She put her hand to her forehead, already pacing the floor. "Leave it to Rusty to mess things up! First by sticking his nose in where it didn't belong, then by getting himself killed!"

"I rather doubt he was pleased about that second fact, either," her guest remarked dryly.

"But we've covered all our tracks, right?" she asked, stopping to peer up at him with intense eyes. "There's no way they can prove what we've done, is there?"

"They haven't caught us yet," he pointed out. "We're careful not to leave an obvious trail. We won't use the card numbers we harvested this weekend until later in the year, if not next. By then, they'll have forgotten all about the show, and how we held their wallets for them. They'll have no reason to connect our show with a charge made in east Louisiana, or Abilene, or wherever it is we head next."

"I don't know," she said, still looking worried. "Yesterday, when we did that bit with the trap door… That fat man didn't want to hand over his wallet for safe-keeping."

"But you convinced him it might fall out of his pocket when he crawled through. And it's a good thing he handed it over, too. He had a platinum card, no limit."

"But he's likely to remember the incident. He was clearly skeptical about the whole thing to begin with."

"You worry too much. It's going to be fine. We've gotten away with it this long, and we'll continue to get away with it."

"Rusty was getting suspicious. What if he told someone else? What if that someone killed him, and now he or she plans to blackmail us with the information?"

"I think you're giving Rusty too much credit. I don't think he was that smart. I think he was on to us as a couple, not as a team."

She blew out a long, resigned breath. "I just wanted to collect my money and get out of this town. My brother's interference put a real kink in things. If he hadn't come up with that cockamamie scheme—"

"Which failed miserably," her companion was quick to point out.

"How were we to know the lawyer would ride to the rescue? He planned to do that, which would have ingratiated him with her rich uncle. Now, he's forced to use Plan B."

"Which is his project, not ours," he reminded her darkly. "And now, we're stuck here, and you can bet he'll suck us into his latest scheme."

He started for the door but stopped. "One thing, before I go. Did your brother have anything to do with Rusty's death?"

Her answer was slow in coming. "No. No, of course not."

"You're sure about that?"

She didn't quite meet his eyes as she hedged, "You know him. What do you think?"

"I think we're in trouble."

CHAPTER 22

Team Hannah marched toward the show area, but if they expected to make a grand entrance, they were sadly disappointed.

The area was in shambles again, reminding Hannah of the chaos of that first day. The crew was in the middle of disassembling the revolving grandstand. The temporary arena was already down. Only half the string of faux storefronts still stood. Shuddered and dark, the carnival trailers didn't look nearly as festive now. Busy with their tasks, no one looked up as Hannah and Walker approached.

"We'll be lucky to find Jazz in all this mess," Hannah mumbled.

"Look for the steam. The sheriff's already been here with the news, so I figure there should be steam coming from her ears about now."

"I'm glad Tracey Ann called us to let us know. Although with them banned from leaving town, that means we're stuck with them for a few more days."

"At least it gives the sheriff time to look into Rusty's death."

"But if it turns out he was killed, that means there's a murderer among them. Here. On my land, practically in my backyard. And for who knows how long." Hannah shivered at the thought, reaching into her pocket to finger the leather pouch. She wasn't sure she believed in such, but it gave her a measure of comfort.

Walker stopped in his tracks and stared at her.

"What?" she asked defensively. "It's only natural for me to be concerned!"

"It's not that. It's something you said. Hang on, I need to go back to the truck and look at the contract again. You may have given me an idea."

"I want to check on Ladybird one more time. Meet me there."

Finding the horse wasn't as simple as she expected. During the loading process, trucks were moved and trailers lined up, waiting to be loaded. The neat order from previous days was reconfigured, littered with obstacles as big as eighteen-wheelers. Hannah slowly wound her way to the livestock pens, seeing very few workers here in the back. She felt tiny as she walked through the tunnel-like opening between two semi-trucks.

Some of the fences were already down and the horses condensed into as few pens as possible. Only Ladybird had her own space.

Hannah hadn't meant to *visit* the horse so much as to *check* on it. From a distance.

Injured or not, the horse was still huge. Not to mention the mare had gone crazy on her, bucking and taking her on that wild ride. However, Ladybird looked so docile now, standing there munching on alfalfa hay. She was a fashion statement in neat wrappings of turquoise and brown, custom made and monogrammed for a special touch. Hannah had difficulty reconciling the innocent-looking equine with the runaway beast from yesterday.

The dapple held no grudge. She came forward to the fence and nickered again, seeking attention. Hannah hesitantly reached up to stroke her neck.

"Hello, girl," she said bravely. "Hey, I see you're up and moving now. That pretty doctor must have helped you out." She felt immensely relieved, not just for the sake of her own liability, but for the sake of the horse.

The mare bobbed her head, as if agreeing with her. Hannah laughed aloud. "Let's hope there's no real damage, after all." She laughed again as the horse mussed her hair.

The sound of voices floated her way, their angry tones intruding on her cozy moment with Ladybird. The horse tensed and pulled away, reminding Hannah of the sheer power beneath its shiny coat.

Hannah turned around to see where the voices came from. She heard a female voice, sharp and shrill.

"I cannot believe you've jeopardized *my* dream for another of your own selfish schemes!"

The other person's voice was too low for Hannah to hear, but she was certain it belonged to a man.

"I don't care who they are, or how much money you owe them!" Hannah imagined that the woman stomped her foot for emphasis. "You have no right, coming back here and ruining all my hard work! You aren't the only one who worked hard to get where he is. It's taken me years to perfect this act, and in one weekend—one weekend!—you manage to ruin it! Now, I'm stuck here in this hick farce of a town, all because of your greed!"

Curious, Hannah moved forward to get a glimpse of who was talking, but not before she noticed Ladybird had lain down again. *Poor girl. Must be all tuckered out. She's stretched out on her side again.*

The voices came from behind the eighteen-wheelers. Hannah started down the path between the two, thinking to better hear the conversation.

To her dismay, the voices were on the move, receding in the other direction. Hannah glanced down at her watch, wondering what took Walker so long. She turned to retrace her steps, only to find the path was suddenly more crowded.

Guy Woods came up the narrow opening, his bulky frame making the space seem more tunnel-like than ever. Hannah felt a flash of fear as she thought about his quick temper and the speculation surrounding him. Even Pierce said he was a hothead and often fought with his best friend. From what she could tell, he had more reason than anyone to kill Rusty.

"What are you doing back here?" he asked. His tone was less than cordial.

"Uhm…looking for Jazz."

"I'd steer clear of her, if I was you," he warned. "She's on the war path right now. Someone called the police, said one of us killed ole Rusty. Now, we're stuck here." His face contorted in anger. "If we're stuck here, we can't do our next show. No show means no pay. No pay means my bills don't get paid. If I knew who called the sheriff, I'd…" He balled up one fist and slammed it into his other palm, the sound echoing down the tunneled space.

Biting her lower lip, Hannah debated turning around and fleeing in the other direction. If she stayed rooted to the spot, or went forward to brush past him, she stood the chance of Guy grabbing her and…

And what? She was being paranoid. He couldn't possibly know she was responsible for alerting the sheriff's office. She would simply scoot by him and be on her way.

"Hey," he said gruffly. "What'd you say to Daphne earlier?"

"I—I don't… I didn't… n—nothing!" she stammered. "I didn't say anything to her."

"Then why's she giving me the cold shoulder all of a sudden? And asking me questions about Rusty?"

"What kind of questions?"

He shrugged his thick shoulders. "About how I found him, and if we'd had another argument. Some such nonsense about a *tumbled* relationship, whatever the heck that means."

Hannah's quick denial squeaked from her throat. "No idea."

He shook his head with a disgruntled snort. "That woman drives me plumb insane, but there's nothing I wouldn't do for her."

Did that include murder?

Hannah inched her way backward.

"Why'd you go and get that Long fella a job?" he suddenly demanded. "It should have gone to my brother!"

Hannah shook her head, too nervous to verbally deny his accusation. She took another step of retreat.

"Jeff needs that raise. He's been thinkin' of buying a ring for some little gal he's met. He won't tell me who she is, but she's bound to be special. I've never seen my little brother so nervous over a girl." He looked slightly amused, until he glowered and jabbed a finger in her direction. "Now, you robbed him of the raise."

"Not—Not me. I had nothing to do with it."

"That's not the way Jeff sees it. He says you made Jazz hire Long because he's your boyfriend."

Hannah's mind worked overtime. Pieces of previous conversations swirled in her head.

…those *Hats Off* crew are real characters…

…Most have criminal records…

…Two brothers have records of domestic abuse and battery…

…Guy's a hothead…

…harmless. Mostly…

…Guy found out—not about his brother, thank God…

…a murder!…

…With his hot temper, sometimes Guy scares me…

The overhead sun was warm, but a chill of apprehension pebbled Hannah's skin. *Holy boomtown! Had Guy Wood really murdered Rusty?*

Guy was clearly protective of his younger brother, but would he go as far as killing a man to ensure his happiness? And if that were the case, would he now harm *her*, believing she cost Jeff his promotion? What if the two of them had done it together? Sure, it was crazy, but so was Jeff pursing the very woman his brother was in love with. The whole thing was twisted. The brothers were twisted.

No longer concerned about being discreet, Hannah turned around to flee in the opposite direction of where Guy stood. When she saw Jeff coming from the other end, she knew the two brothers had her trapped.

"Hey, little brother," Guy greeted him. "Here's your chance to have that talk with Miss Duncan."

Hannah whirled back around, trying to judge her best chance of escape. Jeff was younger and more agile, but Guy was no doubt stronger. Did she stand a chance getting past either?

"Just the lady I was looking for," agreed Jeff.

"M—Me? Why were you looking for me?"

"Seeing as we're stuck here for a few days, Talia said you—"

"Talia?" Guy broke in sharply. "You're not seeing *her* again, are you? Tell me *she's* not the one we did all this for!"

Hannah barely heard his brother's denial. She was more focused on what Guy meant by 'all this.' Was he referring to his best friend's murder?

Behind Guy, she saw the long, tall form of Shelton Long amble past. With a cry of happiness, she called his name. "Shelton! Shelton, wait up!"

"Oh, hey, Hannah," he said, backing up. His smile said he was pleased to see her. "What happened to you earlier? You just disappeared on me."

Guy looked angry over the interruption, but she ignored him as she scooted past. She all but ran toward Shelton, her knees wobbling in relief.

Once again, the handsome farrier had come to her rescue.

CHAPTER 23

"You look a might piqued. You okay?" Shelton used his exaggerated country bumpkin accent as he peered down at her.

Wanting to put as much distance between herself and the brothers as possible, Hannah grabbed his arm and all but pulled him along. "I'm worried about Ladybird," she said, knowing that would get his attention.

"You and me both, darlin'. I just don't know what's wrong with her." He looked forlorn. "She won't eat, won't drink, won't even get up and walk."

In a hurry or not, Hannah stumbled in surprise when her feet forgot to walk. She scrunched her face in confusion. "I thought she was recovered. She was standing there eating hay, not ten minutes ago!" Hannah told him.

"That's impossible. Doc says she may not be able to stand."

Eager to prove him wrong, Hannah walked faster, until they were within sight of the horse.

The dapple lie on her side, stomach heaving. She lifted her head, looked at them with sad brown eyes, and laid back down with a pathetic sounding nicker.

"I—I don't understand," Hannah said. "I was just here. She was up and moving around. She even came to the fence so I could pet her!"

"You must be mistaken. Doc says it's nerve damage. She can't walk. Her leg won't move."

"Shelton, I'm telling you, I saw that horse on all four feet!"

His face set in determination. "No, you didn't."

Hannah was completely flabbergasted. She dropped his arm and stood back, planting both her hands on her hips. "Are you seriously going to stand there and call me a liar? I know what I saw, Shelton."

"And I know that my horse is lame. You're mistaken."

Walker returned in time to see the heated standoff. Hannah glared up at the tall horseman, her eyes blazing and her posture stiff. Recognizing that look, he couldn't help but chuckle. Horse boy was in for it now. When Hannah lost her temper, she could be a real firecracker.

Long didn't seem to be concerned with the threat of sparks. He stared down at her, his eyes cold and his face determined.

"What's going on here?" Walker asked. He touched a hand to Hannah's back, letting her know that, no matter what the disagreement was about, he took her side.

"I was here ten minutes ago, and that horse was fine," Hannah said, biting the words off in angry snippets. "She was up on her feet, eating and wanting me to pet her. But Shelton is calling me a liar."

"I didn't say you were lying, I said you were mistaken. Look at her! Just look at Lady! She's obviously in no shape to be standing around eating!"

"Shelton, I know what I saw. Maybe she's like a kid. Maybe this is all a show to get your attention."

"Even the vet said—"

Walker broke in, his voice calm and reasonable. "What did Gaby have to say, Shelton? What was her assessment?"

"She's worried Ladybird may have nerve damage. Perhaps internal injuries. There's *something* that keeps her from getting to her feet!" He glared at Hannah, daring her to contradict him.

"Then call her back out here," Hannah taunted, "because your horse just made a miraculous recovery!"

Shelton slung his arm backward toward the stall. "You call *that* a recovery?"

Five feet of fury stormed up behind them. "What on earth is going on back here?" Jazz demanded. "I can hear you two from a mile away!"

They spoke at once, both adamant in their claim.

"Enough!"

Jazz was small, but her voice boomed with authority. The tiny blonde turned toward the substitute wrangler. "Shelton, has the vet been here today? Is there any change in the mare's condition?"

"None." His jaw worked with emotion.

She turned to the innkeeper. "In that case, Hannah, I have to agree with Mr. Long. I was here when the doctor first examined the horse, and I've examined her, myself. The poor mare is unable to stand. Her feed has remained untouched. We haven't moved her yet, for fear of doing more damage, but this horse is obviously in no condition to do the things you claim."

"I would expect as much from you!" Hannah spat.

Her contemptuous reply left Jazz nonplussed. "Then, it will come as no surprise to you that Mr. Long and I both hold you personally responsible for the injury and condition of this mare. Mr. Long, what would you say your horse was worth?"

"She's not for sale!" he barked sharply. "But considering her fine bloodline, the three world champions she's foaled, her past and potential purse earnings as a championship barrel racer in her own right, not to mention the future foals she may birth, I'd say in the upper range of $300,000."

Hannah gasped aloud. Even Walker cleared his throat at the staggering figure.

"Of course, you can't put a dollar value on sentimental value," Shelton insisted.

"But you can certainly put a dollar amount on medical bills," Jazz pitched in, her manner cool and professional. "Hannah, I imagine your insurance pays only the minimum level of care. Surely, you want better for this poor, suffering animal."

"I don't want her to be in pain," Hannah agreed, wondering where this conversation was heading.

She soon found out. Jazz adopted her businesswoman persona again. No show jargon or slurring of words. Her tone was cool, clipped, and professional. "I'm glad your lawyer is present, because I have a proposition for you. It seems we are all faced with rather unusual and dire circumstances. Hannah, I know your heart was in the right place, trying to salvage the show, but your hasty actions put not only your contract in jeopardy, but also the integrity of this show, the safety of my crew, and, of course, Mr. Long's poor, suffering animal. I—"

"Wait just a minute!" Walker broke in. "How did *Hannah's actions* do any of that?"

"Why, she insisted on using Mr. Long's horse, of course. I was against it. I warned her that it was highly unusual, and that it wouldn't be covered under my insurance policy, but she insisted she would be fully and financially responsible for the animal."

With a frown, Hannah protested, "That wasn't exactly the way it happened."

"It's the way I recall it," Shelton said stubbornly.

"And I'm afraid I have to agree."

No one noticed Pierce's approach, until he spoke in Jazz's defense. The petite blonde flashed him a grateful smile.

"You see? There were only the four of us present, and three of us agree on what actually happened. You, Hannah, insisted we use the horse. You threatened to shut us down if we didn't agree to do things your way."

Seething, Hannah heeded Walker's silent warning to keep quiet.

"And you, Hannah," she continued, "were riding the horse when you lost control and allowed the horse to wreak havoc on the set and consequently sustain serious injury. You assured Mr. Long that you were a skilled horsewoman and could adequately handle a high-spirited horse. However—"

"I did no such thing!" She turned to Shelton with a beseeching look. "Shelton, you know that's not true. Tell them."

"I can't say I recall, either way," he denied. "You said you could ride, and I believed you."

"You told me your horse was a sweetheart!"

"She is."

"Being *your* sweetheart doesn't count!" she snapped. Eyes ablaze, Hannah turned to the one man she could trust. "This is all a set-up, Walker. And now she's pulled Shelton into her scam. And Pierce, too."

Walker put a hand on Hannah's arm. Using the slightest amount of pressure, he silently urged her to trust him. "I believe you have a proposition for us, Ms. Dawson?" His tone was almost bored.

"As I've pointed out, Ms. Duncan is solely responsible for the unfortunate situation we find ourselves in. She's already assumed full financial responsibility for our services, as well as the services and care for the injured animal. It will be a shame, really, to add the additional strain and cost of a lawsuit."

"And what lawsuit is that?" From the deceptive note of calm in Walker's voice, it was impossible to detect his full ire. Hannah, however, stood near enough to feel the tension radiating from the tight coils of his body.

"Why, the ones Mr. Long and *Hats Off* will both be filing, of course. I've already outlined the basis of our argument… reneging on the contract, jeopardizing the integrity of this show, risking the safety of my crew and equipment, and causing serious and quite possibly permanent damage to Mr. Long's horse. Add to that the mental anguish we've all suffered and any lingering consequences resulting from this weekend, and we'll be seeking somewhere in the neighborhood of four to eight million dollars. A piece, of course."

Hannah paled visibly, but Walker never flinched. "I venture to guess you propose a settlement. Am I correct?"

Jazz smiled without humor. "It does seem the most logical thing, don't you agree? It would save everyone a great deal of time, energy, and mental stress. And of course, it would save you, Hannah, a great deal of money."

"What did you have in mind?"

"I would consider settling for one million dollars."

"One *million*?" Hannah croaked.

Shelton was already shaking his head. "I would need more than that. I need adequate care for Ladybird. At least one point five."

"Are you insane?" Hannah hissed. "Where do you think I would get that kind of money? You both have lost your minds!"

"I have a suggestion," Pierce quietly pitched in.

"I just bet you do," Hannah mumbled. "It was your bright idea to use Ladybird, in the first place." Her eyes narrowed in suspicion. "That was all a set-up, too, wasn't it?" she realized.

At least my first impression of him was correct. Cocky and way too self-assured. She found small comfort in the thought.

Pierce neither denied nor confirmed her claim. "I'm sure your uncle will be more than happy to save you from the stress and humiliation involved with a lawsuit. Imagine what something like that could do to your reputation, and the image you're trying to establish for the inn. I know Joe would do anything to spare you that sort of pain." He flashed his most charming smile. "I've seen your uncle win—and lose—that much during one poker game. He can afford it, Hannah."

It suddenly became clear. "So, that's what this is about," Hannah said in understanding. "You saw a way to make a quick buck off my uncle and decided to use me as your bargaining tool."

"I have no idea what you're talking about." Jazz's manner remained cool. "I'm simply seeking compensation for damages you inflicted. How you pay is your concern."

Hannah knew nothing could be further from the truth. "Something that strikes me odd," she pointed out, "is your concern for Mr. Long's horse, when it really has nothing to do with you."

"Of course, it does! Not only did Ladybird's injury have a direct and profound impact on the show, but it had an impact on our family. As I've told you before, we're one big family here at *Hats Off*. Mr. Long and his horse are now part of that family, if only for a short while. When one of us is suffering, we all feel the pain."

"Oddly enough," Walker noted coolly, "the horse's injury seems to have had a greater impact on you than the death of your crew member. Strange sense of family you have, Ms. Dawson."

She stiffened immediately. "We are deeply saddened by Rusty's passing."

"Not to mention furious that the sheriff has detained you, insisting you not leave town," Hannah put in.

"You know, speaking of that…" Walker reached into his shirt pocket and pulled out a folded sheet of paper. "This is for you, Ms. Dawson."

"A check?" she asked hopefully.

"Not quite. It's a bill."

She frowned. "Whatever for?"

"Does your 'vacate the premises' clause ring a bell, Ms. Dawson?"

For the first time during the encounter, Jazz looked less than confident. "What about it?" she snapped.

Hannah turned to him with a question in her eyes.

"The reason I went back to the truck," Walker told her. His dark eyes twinkled with mirth. "According to their own contract, they have to vacate the premises in 'a fast and efficient exit.' It's a selling point, actually, so Jazz goes the extra mile and gives herself not only a strict deadline, but a self-imposed fine for not meeting it." He made a show of consulting his wristwatch. "You have thirty-two minutes remaining, Ms. Dawson. Think you can have everything packed and gone in that time?"

"Of course not!' she snapped. "The sheriff has ordered us to stay in place."

"And as you may recall, if you remain on the premises in excess of twenty-four hours after the last performance, you must pay the venue twice their normal rental fee."

"We have a rental fee?" Hannah squeaked in surprise. "For our pasture?"

"Actually," he said, pulling another sheet from his pocket, "we do have a fee. I had to give it a monetary value, for insurance purposes. Remember, Jazz? You insisted we carry an insurance policy in case of inclement weather or other natural causes. And you asked me to list the property high, in case we had to rent an alternate location."

Hannah gasped when she saw the number on the paper. "She'll have to pay me *double* that amount?"

"Absolutely."

"But we're under sheriff's order to remain! It's out of our hands."

"I thought you might say that, so I checked the contract. There were no exclusions and no allowances. If my calculations are correct, if you're detained by two days, it should equal the full booking fee you're demanding from my client. Factor in today's late penalty, and any additional days it may take the sheriff to clear this matter up, and you could very well owe Hannah, rather than the other way around."

Jazz did not take the news well, but to her credit, she didn't make a scene. Her face underwent several color transformations, changing from an alarming shade of white to a sickly green, before tinting a bright, blotchy red. She seethed quietly for several moments, then took a deep breath and steeled herself for a new proposition.

"I could point out that since the contract is now null and void, we are no longer bound to the terms of agreement. However, I want to be fair." Her smile was too stiff to be convincing. "I propose that we call it even. You don't owe us for our services, and we don't owe you for the rental. We'll consider it a wash."

Walker spoke before Hannah had the opportunity. "We'll take your offer under consideration."

"But—"

"There's no rush, Hannah," he reminded her. "We'll consider the offer. In the meantime, let's discuss the lawsuit."

At the confident look in the attorney's eyes—there was almost a smirk upon his face—Jazz was immediately on the defensive. "You can't expect us to back down on that," she demanded. "Mr. Long's horse was seriously injured."

"Yes, I believe you may have mentioned that a few dozen times."

His tone was so cavalier, and so smug, even Hannah jerked his way. She was surprised to hear his callous concern for the injured animal. Her frown deepened when she saw the way his eyes darted to the horse's pen, subtly urging her to follow his gaze.

Shelton, too, took offense at the comment. While the horse owner launched into a heated rant, Hannah sneaked a peek at the pen behind him. The mare still lay on her side, a sad and sorry sight to behold. It didn't take an expert to see that the horse was in bad shape.

But it wasn't the horse that widened Hannah's eyes in surprise. It was the fact that the horse was no longer alone in the corral. Both Gouyen and Orlan Varela stood inside, peering down at the prone animal. While Hannah watched, Gouyen squatted down, legs spread wide, to bend over the mare's head. The ghost's hand floated two inches above the horse's face, the tattered edges of her clothing superimposing over Ladybird's ear.

To Hannah's surprise, the horse's ear twitched.

The ghost floated over the animal and leaned down to repeat the process along its injured leg.

Another tickle of fabric, another twitch. The leg that 'won't move' kicked as if to swat a fly.

Orlan flashed a big smile and a thumbs up signal.

"Uhm, so let me get this straight." Hannah abruptly broke into whatever claims Shelton still made. She didn't bother looking at him, even as he sputtered to a stop and glared at her. "The lawsuit is based on the fact that Mr. Long's horse was injured," she confirmed, "and not on the fact that I supposedly broke my contract."

"Primarily, yes," the other woman agreed. "The injury is the driving force behind the damages we'll both seek."

"So if the horse made a miraculous recovery…"

"Which, unfortunately, isn't the case."

"I'm not so sure about that," Hannah said, gazing pointedly into the pen. She even stepped over a few feet, to have a non-obstructive view. "In fact, I'm feeling pretty optimistic."

Walker shared her amused smile. "You know what? So am I."

Jazz, Pierce, and Shelton all turned to see what held Hannah's fascination. They couldn't see the old medicine woman making a full circle around the horse. They didn't see the way she knelt in the hay beside the mare's head. They saw only the horse, lying perfectly still except for an occasional twitch of her ear and the quick, nervous blink of her eye. They saw nothing to inspire such optimism in their companions.

They saw the horse lift her head, shake it as if to shake away a fly, and lay it back down again. The act was unremarkable and nothing new. It wasn't the mare's neck that was injured.

Only Hannah and Walker saw Gouyen lean over a second time. This time, she whispered something directly into the horse's ear. Amazingly, the horse tried to sit up.

"Lady!" Shelton shouted.

When the horse lay back down, the old ghost persisted. She again whispered in its ear. This time when the horse sat up, Orlan slipped onto her back. He kneed the animal in the flank, yelled 'giddy up' and—though Shelton and the vet both said it couldn't be done—the mare scrambled to her feet.

"Lady!" Shelton barked again.

The horse looked uncertain, swaying unsteadily on her feet. When Gouyen slapped her ghostly hand onto the animal's rump, a tiny puff of dust floated in the air. She said something more to the horse, her tone sharp and urgent. The horse responded by standing at attention, her eyes wide and unblinking. She was clearly frightened.

Orlan swept off his broad-brimmed hat and bowed in a grand manner, his smile wide.

"I—I don't understand," Jazz stammered.

Hannah's smile was smug. "You were right, Jazz. It's all about trickery. Obviously, this horse has been trained to do tricks."

"Now, wait just a cotton-pickin' minute!" Shelton bellowed. "Just because she's able to stand doesn't prove a thing. She could still be weak and crippled. She hasn't even taken a step yet." Turning back to the horse, he opened his mouth to bark out her name again.

Before he could utter a sound, the ghostly vaquero pulled a trick of his own. He pressed his ghostly knees into the horse's sides and trotted her smartly around the pen for two full turns. As their pace quickened, the horse's eyes grew wider and more frantic. The highly skilled horse had no training for what was happening now. There were no ghosts in her portfolio of tricks.

Orlan released a series of spirited yips. Terrified, the mare sailed over the fence with ease, clearing the top rung with feet to spare. She galloped full speed away, desperate to rid herself of the unwanted rider. The ghost floated just above the blanket, left hand held high, and having the time of his life. (Or death, as the case were.) He twirled his lasso in the air and taunted the horse to buck him off. After two unsuccessful attempts, the animal quietened. Orlan calmed the horse down, turned her back toward their audience, and brought her to a stop several feet away. He bowed again for his magnificent performance.

Clapping, Hannah couldn't resist a burst of laughter at the vaquero's antics. The twinkling sound overrode Shelton's muttered string of curse words and Jazz's blubbering attempt to salvage the situation. Walker snagged his arm around Hannah's waist and enjoyed a rumble or two of laughter, himself.

Hannah darted a glance back toward the medicine woman, but her image had already disappeared. Either her work here was done, or she had expelled all her energy. Even Orlan had faded away.

"It appears your mare experienced a miraculous recovery, horse boy." Walker made only a half-hearted attempt not to gloat.

Shelton had his back to them as he stared at his horse. He hadn't run to the animal's aid, as Hannah had expected, or checked for injuries. Instead, he stood with splayed legs and heaving chest, his hands balled at his sides.

"Don't think this is over," he said in a thick, gravelly voice. His voice was loud enough, steely enough, to easily carry over his turned back. "I've gone too far to turn back now. It's all, or nothing."

Something in his voice wiped the humor from Walker's face. He glanced down at Hannah, who had heard the same thing and shared his concern. It was the sound of desperation. The sound of a man with nothing left to lose. Walker's arm tightened on Hannah's waist, and he tugged her slightly behind him in a protective gesture, even before Shelton turned slowly around.

Even before they saw the gun in his hand.

CHAPTER 24

"What are you doing?"

Jazz's voice broke the stillness. The stifling silence hung over them like an invisible curtain, shielding them, nonetheless, from their surroundings. They stood in the midst of busyness, yet they were apart from it all.

Around them, horses nickered from their crowded pens, while lambs huddled together into one corner of theirs. In the not-so-far distance, *Hats Off* cast and crew scurried back and forth with their tasks, unconcerned with whatever was happening near the livestock pens. Even if they could see past the eighteen-wheelers, they would assume it was another of Jazz's rants, or some such drama between her and lover-boy. It was nothing new, nothing worth interrupting their work.

"Put the gun away. Let's be sensible," Pierce agreed.

Shelton shook his head, his brown eyes bright with nervous energy. "It's no use, Jazz. I can't back down now. I need that money."

"We'll find another way. We always do. Please, David, just put down the gun."

Hannah's head swiveled toward the blond pixie. "David? Shelton is your *brother*?"

Jazz took her eyes off the armed man just long enough to look Hannah's way and nod. "David Shelton Long-Dawson. When our parents divorced, he and Mom both dropped the Dawson." Her eyes went back to her brother. Her eyes, and her voice, were filled with sorrow. "Come on, David. Don't do something we'll both regret."

"It's not too late, Long," Walker spoke out, his voice authoritative, but oddly gentle. He might have been speaking to a skittish horse. "No harm's been done, not really. We can spin it as a prank gone bad. Trickery."

"He's right," Jazz urged, taking a few tentative steps forward. "Give me the gun. It's not too late to stop this foolishness."

"It is! It is too late!" Shelton waved the gun, pointing to no one in particular. His Adam's apple worked up and down, bobbing nervously in the bony column of his throat. "Don't you see? I've already killed a man!"

With a collective gasp, the four people in front of him froze. Walker was the first to move, sweeping his hand behind him to ensure Hannah was safe and securely tucked behind him. Jazz moved next, shrinking back in a reversal of her steps. Pierce stood rooted to the spot, his dark face sallow.

"K—Killed a man? Wh—Who—What are you talking about?" Jazz asked.

"I had to find a way into the show. Don't you see?" His voice took on the whine of nervousness. "A way that wouldn't make them suspect you and I were related, that we were working together."

"We weren't working together, David. Not until you rooted your way in." There was an edge to her voice.

A trace of resentment. "Not until you forced *your* horse into *my* show."

"Exactly. That's exactly why I did it!" His eyes had gone from nervous to wild. "I needed a way in. A way to turn this to both our advantage."

Her face filled with disbelief. "So, you killed Rusty? Is that how you found a way in? Why? Why, David! Why would you *do* that?" Tears streamed down her face as she threw herself into Pierce's arms and sobbed.

"Don't you dare judge me!" Shelton raged. "We've both done plenty we weren't proud of. It's what our father taught us to do. All those shows we did when we were kids. They were nothing but a cover-up for Dad. He was using us, so he could pull his own scams."

"He taught us to cheat, yes. To steal. To trick people out of their money." She shook her head so hard, her blond curls swung in the air. "But not to kill. Never that."

Seeing the disappointment in his sister's eyes, the sorrow, his voice took on a desperate edge again. "You don't understand. I have to get that money. Salvidor put pressure on me. He threatened to hurt Mom again, if I didn't pay up. When I found out you were coming to my town, I had to find a way in. I knew you would help me. You always do."

Despite his pale color, Pierce found his voice. "Salvidor? Vegas' biggest mob boss?"

Pushing out of his arms, Jazz glared up at her brother. "What do you mean, hurt Mom? *Again*?"

Shelton, aka David, swallowed hard. His Adam's apple danced again. "That wreck she had last year…"

"When she had the blowout?"

"It may not have been an accident."

"Why you—" When Jazz would have stormed him, Pierce grabbed her arm and held her in place.

"My brother," she spat, her words directed to no one in particular, "has a weakness for gambling. Unfortunately, he's no better at it than he is at paying his debts. This isn't the first time he's gotten in over his head and come running to me for help. But, I *swear*," she threw these words directly at her brother, along with daggers from her eyes, "it is the last. Never again, David. We're done." She turned her back on the tall man, only to whirl back around and scream, "Do you hear me, David? We. Are. Done."

"Fine. *Little sister,*" he taunted. Hard lines etched into his face.

Had she really ever thought him handsome, Hannah wondered. Twisted in anger, his face was a study in evil.

Evil. Her fingers found the leather pouch in her pocket. Caressing the ancient hide, she wondered why Gouyen hadn't stayed for the final reveal. She had shown Hannah only part of Shelton's true colors.

"That's fine," he continued. "And it's just as well. This way, I don't have to share. Because, for the first time, I have an ace in the hole."

"No more scams, Shelton. David. Whatever your name is," Pierce said. He held the devastated Jazz in his arms as he glared at her brother. "For once in your life, man up and take responsibility for yourself."

"I'm taking something else." With a cold smile, Shelton made a motion with his gun. "Hannah, step out here."

Walker leaned back so quickly, his shoulders smacked Hannah in the face. She spat out a mouthful of shirt as a buzz started in her ears. Either Walker bumped her harder than he intended, or she was hearing things. The blood rushed through her head like a humming motor, almost drowning out the words, but she could have sworn she heard Shelton tell her to come forward.

"Hannah's not going anywhere."

This, she heard. And felt. The growled words rumbled through Walker's chest and vibrated against her cheek.

"I say she is. I have no doubt Joseph Duncan will pay a nice ransom to get his precious niece back in one piece. Hannah, come out here."

"You touch one hair on her head, and Salvidor will be the least of your worries, horse boy."

Shelton laughed at the lawyer's threat. "I think you forget. I'm the one with the gun." He waved it for emphasis. "Not that I've needed it, all the times in the past. Haven't you learned by now, book boy? I can beat you any day, any way."

Walker didn't hesitate to issue a challenge. "Prove it. Put the gun down, and put your money where your mouth is." He took a step forward, even though Hannah literally clung to him. His shirt balled into her hands. He tried to shake her free as he leveled his eyes on the other man in a blatant dare. "Like Maldonado said. Man up."

He was tempted. Hesitation hummed in the air. The farrier clearly itched to fight his long-standing opponent and prove his superiority, once and for all. Winner take all. In this case, it would be Hannah. A woman Walker obviously cared for. A woman who would make Shelton an extremely wealthy man.

Shelton forced himself to focus. "No deal, book boy," he drawled.

The hum grew louder, and for the first time, Hannah realized it was real.

She shouldn't have been surprised to see the golf cart bouncing along the trampled grass of the makeshift arena, weaving in and out of the trailers and piles of equipment. Leave it to Sadie, Fred, and Leroy to save the day. They approached from the far side, which meant they had to have circled the scene to approach from behind. With his back to them, Shelton never saw the sport utility vehicle dart up the path Ladybird had recently taken. Its quiet motor was nothing more than a hum, easily drowned out by the sounds around them, particularly the collective sound of their pounding hearts.

Sadie drove, while Fred got into position. Dressed in her customary pressed western duds, red-felt cowboy hat, and her oversized sweetheart belt buckle, she wasn't riding a horse, but she had her rope. Holding on with one arm, Fred hung half out of the cart, swirling the rope high and wide. It made a curious swooshing sound, one that drew Shelton's attention.

The armed gunman looked up, but not behind him. And not in time. When Fred gave the signal, Sadie tooted the cart's horn. From the backseat, Leroy gave one sharp bark of warning. By the time the man whirled around, the rope was already looped around his shoulders. Fred let it fall to his elbows before she gave the lasso a sharp whip, cinching it tight to effectively bind his arms against his sides. The gun fell useless to the ground.

Walker rushed in, snatching the gun and tossing the bound man onto the ground. When Fred threw him her end of the rope, he quickly used it to tie Shelton's feet.

Had the golf cart been a horse and Shelton a calf, they would have had a record-breaking time at calf roping.

"You blew it, horse boy," Walker said, his breath heaving from the effort of restraining the other man. The huge white Great Pyrenees acted as backup, standing sentry over the prone body on the ground. "You should have taken my challenge." He grinned up at the beaming elderly sisters. "You stood a better chance with me, than you ever did against these two."

CHAPTER 25

By Wednesday, the tiny hamlet of Hannah was quiet again. With no guests booked for the inn until the next day, the rambling old space was blessedly still. The only guests in residence were the Elliott family, booked in the Anheim Cabin for the entire week.

Hannah used the downtime to rest. There were a hundred and thirty-two items on her three To-Do lists, but for the moment, she ignored them all. Guilt nibbled at her conscience for neglecting her duties, but she reasoned that she was taking care of something equally important: her sanity.

They were having one of their too-rare gatherings down by the pond. A full moon hung in the inky sky, offering just the right ambiance for the meal. While Walker grilled fat, juicy pork chops to perfection, Hannah and Sadie set up the card table and brought out the rest of the meal. Fred gathered firewood and built a small fire. It was more for looks than warmth, as the temperature was mild on this late spring night in Texas.

They finished the meal with Sadie's famous macaroons and a couple of bottles of Fred's 'special reserve' wine. Made from the mustang grapes that grew in abundance around the property, it was one of her best batches yet, but she reserved it for special occasions and special friends. Tonight qualified on both accounts.

"To Team Hannah." They tipped their red plastic cups together as Hannah made the toast. "I'm getting us all t-shirts, by the way, that have that on them. I want everyone to know that's what we are. A team."

As they sipped the sweet, tangy wine, Hannah took the opportunity to thank them all, yet again. "I know I've said it before, but it bears repeating. I owe so much to all three of you. Not just for this weekend, but for all the days leading up to it. Despite the fiasco at the end, we had a successful grand opening, and we accomplished all the goals we set. I couldn't ask for a better support team than the one I have. So, again. Thank you."

"We did do a pretty fine job, didn't we?" Fred preened from her folding chair.

"I truly couldn't have done it without you. All three of you have gone above and beyond." She reached down to pat the big dog lounging at her feet. "Make that the four of you."

"I think you may be giving me more credit than due," Walker said. "You three did all the heavy lifting." He held his cup up in tribute. "Ladies."

"Don't be modest, Walker. I know you were conveniently absent when all the painting was going on." Hannah gave him a stern look, but it softened as she continued, "But when it came down to it, you were there for me. You stood between a gun and me. That's nothing to shake off lightly."

"There was no way I was going to let that man take you with him." His voice was gruff, still raw with the memory of the danger of that day. "Not as long as I was breathing."

"I'm glad it didn't come to that," she said softly. She tried to express her gratitude through her eyes, but how did she adequately thank him for something like that?

The look between them was a live current, carrying in the night air like an electric wave.

Walker broke the connection by clearing his throat and looking down into his cup. "Thanks to these two, it didn't have to." He lifted it again, this time to the two women sitting between him and Hannah. "Thanks to their quick thinking, they easily defused the situation."

"Orlan showed up at the inn, hootin' and hollarin' about his great ride," Fred recalled, shaking her head. "We couldn't quite make out what he was saying about proving the tall man was a liar—"

"But when Gouyen showed up—" Sadie broke in.

"She doesn't normally do that, you know," reminded Fred.

"—we knew something was happening. She just grunted and motioned for us to follow. Leroy was yapping and trying to lead the way. The golf cart was parked at the back door, so we jumped in and followed. I left the back door wide open and all the ingredients for my pie right there on the counter!" Sadie threw her hands up in a show of abandon. "But that old woman and Leroy kept urging us forward, and then, we saw he had a gun!"

Fred took over the story. "I thought she had lost her mind, but Sadie darted the cart to the left, before he got a good look at us. She made a wide swing around the backside of the pens and came up behind him, in his blind spot. I spotted the rope there on the floor of the golf cart and knew what I had to do."

Sadie beamed at her sister. "You've still got it, old gal."

Fred brushed off the compliment. "Walker, I think you and I should think about doing some calf roping together. We'd make a heck of a team."

The lawyer simply laughed. "I think I'll just stick with my day job. And my duties with Team Hannah. They both keep me plenty busy."

"Sister, I hate to leave good company—" Sadie began.

"—but we should go," Fred finished. She was already up and gathering their belongings. "You two don't rush on our account. There's still half a bottle of wine, and the fire's not quite out yet."

"I'll take care of it before I go," Walker promised. Even beside a pond, it wasn't safe to leave embers unattended, much less an open flame.

"Can we switch chairs? That one's ours."

"Sure. Here, let me get these for you." Walker stood and folded the vacated chair, then loaded it alongside its mate into the back of the golf cart. The rest was already stowed in his truck for transport back to the inn.

By the time the sisters and Leroy were gone, and Walker had settled into the remaining chair, the woman beside him was quiet.

"I can hear you thinking, all the way over here," he said.

"All three inches away? Sorry, I'll think quieter."

"Or louder," he suggested. "I didn't quite make out that last thought."

Her chuckle was short-lived. "Sure, you did. I was thinking I'll have another glass of wine."

He poured the last of the rich-colored liquid into both their cups, giving her the larger portion.

"You trying to get me tipsy?" she accused with an arched brow.

"After these last few days, I figure you deserve it."

Hannah took a long draw before dropping her head back against the chair and consulting the stars. The vast night sky was as dark as her thoughts.

After a space of several silent moments, Walker spoke. "None of us saw it, you know. Quit beating yourself up."

She didn't pretend not to understand his meaning. "I keep thinking how could I have been so blind?"

"We all were. We knew him longer than you did. He had lived and worked among us for almost three years. None of us suspected he was capable of murder. And you heard how hard Fred took it. It completely destroyed some theory she had. Something about a man treating a woman the way he treats his horse." He shrugged his broad shoulders, not quite certain of the exact claim.

"But you warned me, Walker. You warned me not to trust him. Not to be fooled by his good looks and his country-boy charm. And as it turned out, he wasn't a country boy at all. Born and raised in Las Vegas. He learned about horses from his rodeo bum father and from working backstage at stage shows and rodeos. Even the Texas accent was fake."

Walker frowned but nodded in agreement. "I always thought it was a little thick."

"You told me to stay away from him, but I thought you were just being—" She stopped herself before she said something foolish. She hadn't had so much wine that she didn't know when to keep her mouth closed.

"Mean?" he supplied.

"That's not what I was going to say."

"Then what?"

She hesitated, taking another sip of wine as she stalled. It was one sip closer to loosening her tongue.

"What, Hannah? Why did you think I told you to stay away from Long?"

"I thought you were jealous." There. She had blurted it out. When the words just sat there, hanging in the air without merit, without welcome, she hurried to say, "I know. I was being foolish."

"You weren't." His words were low and hard to hear, even though they sat side by side. They were even harder to say. Walker swallowed and made the admission, "I was jealous."

"Yeah, but of Gabriella. I totally misread the situation."

He rubbed the back of his neck. "About Gabriella…"

"You don't have to say anything. I get it. She's a beautiful woman. Friendly and smart, and very likable. And apparently honest. She seemed truly appalled by Shelton's scam. I believed her when she said she had no idea he had trained the horse to act injured."

She shook her head, still trying to wrap her head around the depths of Shelton Long's desperation. "I still can't believe he deliberately did that to his horse. He put the wrong size shoe on her feet, knowing it would be painful for her stand. He knew she would stay off her feet as much as possible, playing into the act of being hurt. Did you catch the way Shelton called her Lady during that time, instead of Ladybird? I think that was one of the cues for the trick. No wonder Gabriella suspected nerve damage." She was rambling, she knew, but it was the best way to salvage her pride. Because she *did* get it. What man wouldn't be attracted to the vivacious vet?

Unlike her, Walker stayed focused on the topic at hand. He continued as if she hadn't spoken.

"I know I accused Gaby of siding with Shelton during the trial, but I realize now I shouldn't have. I always knew she was trustworthy. She's a consummate professional. She would never lie, and never jeopardize the health or safety of an animal. This episode proved that, and it forced me to go back to look at the facts from before. She didn't lie under oath. She answered the questions as they were asked. I should have done a better job on the cross-examine. That one's on me."

Hannah had no idea about the details of the case, but she knew it took a big man to admit when he was wrong. She admired his candor, even if it meant heartache for her. No doubt, he and the veterinarian would get back together now.

"I hope you told her that."

"I did. We had a long talk, and I'd like to think we made things right between us again. Gaby's been a good friend to me."

"And with Shelton out of the picture, you can go back to being more than friends." She tried to sound cheerful, but suspected she failed miserably. She felt a physical pain, right in the area of her heart, at the thought of losing him.

Not that she had ever had him to begin with.

"It's true; we did date for a short time. But long before horse boy came into the picture, we decided we did best as friends. We weren't ever really an item."

"Then, why were you jealous?"

"Why do you think?" It wasn't a direct answer, but it went a long way to lessen some of the ache in Hannah's heart. This whole conversation about Gabriella had it smarting like an open gash.

Hannah stared into the dying fire. "I don't know what to think anymore," she answered glumly. "Apparently, I'm a horrible judge of character. Not just with Shelton, but with everyone. I actually suspected Guy and Jeff of killing Rusty. I thought they were the brothers with the domestic assault records. I thought Jeff wanted to threaten me, when all he wanted to know was where to find a local jewelry store.

"I thought Ted and Tom were the nice ones," she continued, "and that it was noble of Ted to stay behind with his brother, rather than pursuing his talents in Nashville. Little did I know, they both have criminal backgrounds! And I truly *liked* Pierce, once I got to know him better. Which proved I never really knew him, at all." Her sigh was long and heartfelt.

"He and Jazz had a nice little scam going, stealing people's personal information when they volunteered for skits. The amazing thing is how they had gotten away with it for so long. And they still would be, if Shelton hadn't come along and spoiled things."

"I can't believe he kissed me," she muttered thickly. She scrubbed the back of her hand against her lips. "He'd already killed a man by then. A murderer actually kissed me!" She scrubbed harder. "And I let him. Well, not exactly, because he just grabbed me. But I didn't stop him. I—"

"He grabbed you?"

"Well, not like *attack* grab," she admitted. "I was blabbering about something—you, I think, and how I should call you, which he said was a bit of an insult, since he had just asked me out—and he was trying to shut me up, so he grabbed me and kissed me."

A small smile worked around the corners of Walker's mouth. "I can see where that might be a blow to his ego."

Hannah stared into the embers, watching the low flames flicker and wane. "It was just more of his trickery," she murmured.

Walker stared with her into the glowing cinders. Both were mesmerized by the steady tempo of the flames. Even though it danced to the tune of certain death, the fire surged and pulsed, retreating within itself to simmer among the live embers, only to build once again into a blazing crescendo. The hiss and crackle created a beat of its own, working its way into their heads, insinuating its hum into the very beat of their hearts.

"A man shouldn't use trickery to kiss a woman." Walker spoke the words after a long moment. The words were thoughtful, almost spoken in monotone. "If he wants to kiss her, he should say so."

Hannah made a murmur of agreement.

"That's something I thought about," he went on, "when Long had us at gunpoint." His tone took on a faint philosophical air. "I kept thinking I blew my best chance. I should have kissed you when I had the chance."

It took a few moments for the words to penetrate the tune in her head. She was still trapped within the fire's trance, her blood pulsing with the heady orchestra drumming through her veins.

"Wait. What?" She turned to look at him in surprise.

His eyes were still drawn to the dying flames. The glowing embers worked like a truth serum, pulling his deepest, darkest thoughts out into the open. "It was right here at this pond," he mumbled. "I had a chance to kiss you, but I took the easy way out. I used a trick of my own. I hid behind the thin veil of propriety, and some nonsense about being your lawyer. About having your best interests at heart."

"I remember."

Her soft comment broke his concentration. He turned to her, as if just now remembering she sat by his side, their chairs butted up against the other. He looked at her for a long moment, watching the weak flicker of light play there in the shadows of her face.

Neither spoke. Through the space of a dozen or more heartbeats—a full stanza of the fire's hum—they stared at one another in honest assessment.

Walker was the first to break the silence. "I want to kiss you, Hannah." His words were soft, but blunt. "No tricks. No gimmicks." He blinked, revealing the first hint of his vulnerability. "No lies." His gaze dropped briefly to her lips, then back to her eyes. "Just an honest kiss."

"I'd like that," she whispered.

Holding her gaze, Walker leaned forward. Her eyes fluttered closed as his mouth settled upon hers, warm and steady. His kiss was neither soft, nor hard. It was the weight of shared exploration, the perfect pressure of give and take. Slow and deliberate, the kiss wasn't too long, nor was it too short.

It was, Hannah thought with a breathy sigh of happiness as they slowly pulled apart, *simply perfect.*

They shifted in their chairs, so that his arms circled around her and she could lay her head back against his shoulder. Staring into what was left of the fire—and stoking it once or twice to revive the flame—they were in no hurry to end this perfect moment in time. Beneath the dark canopy of night sky, it was just the two of them, forging together into the unknown.

"Now what?" Hannah whispered after a while. For once in her life, her mind didn't race ahead with a ticker tape of ideas. She was strangely content with not knowing what lay ahead.

"I don't know." His reply was honest. When she turned to look up at him, Hannah saw the light of the fire reflecting in his stormy blue eyes. It was a pale comparison to the glow she saw within. "I don't know what's next. But I'd like to find out."

"So would I," she whispered.

A slow smile stretched across Walker's handsome face, and his arms tightened around her. Another gentle kiss, and they turned back to watch the fire, mesmerized once again by the slow crackle and burn of the glowing coals. Lost in the come-hither dance of the low flames, they both knew that strong relationships were like banked fires.

To stand the test of time, some things needed to simmer.

Note from Author

Join us again soon, for the next installment of *Spirits of Texas Cozy Mysteries!*

Thank you for reading my tale. If you enjoyed it, please share your thoughts on the platform(s) of your choice. Oftentimes, readers underestimate the power of a review, but just a few lines can make a huge difference in a book's—and author's—success.

After leaving your review, please write to me at beckiwillis.ccp@gmail.com. I'd love to e-visit with you!

www.beckiwillis.com

ABOUT THE AUTHOR

As an avid reader herself, Becki Willis likes to write about believable characters in believable situations. Many of her books stem from personal experiences. (No worries; she's never actually murdered anyone.) She's won several awards, but the real compliments come from her readers. Becki loves spending time with her family, unraveling a good mystery, traveling, dark chocolate, and strong coffee.